1980
"THE YEAR THE PAST DISAPPEARED"

SHANE O'BRIEN MACDONALD

Ankerville Street Productions
North America

Copyright © 2014 Shane O'Brien MacDonald

First digital edition September 2014
ISBN: 978-0-9920080-8-6
First trade paperback edition September 2014
ISBN: 978-0-9920080-9-3

Found an error in one of our books?
Don't get angry, get us to fix it! Contact us:
Ankerville Street Productions North America
ankervillestreetprods@gmail.com

Cover design by Yukiko Sato

From inside the novel...

"Spare me the speech. The plan's in motion. There's no way to stop me."

"You're going to blow the top off this mountain?"

Dewey laughed. "No, I'm going to blow up the crust of the earth under Los Angeles. Let it catch fire. I suppose you had time to examine the tools where I left you the last time."

"Yeah, but—"

"Next to that conveyor belt is a bore hole. Reaching down twenty-five kilometers into the earth. It's super hot. That's where the bomb will drop, hitting terminal velocity in a vacuum, once the air is sucked out of the hole."

"What is this?" said Rock. "Some kind of science experiment?"

"The computer simulation—"

"Bullshit. You have no idea what you're doing. That bomb won't destroy anything underground. The Soviets have been doing this for almost a century."

"Don't be so sure."

"Tell me, did you create the tsunami, too?"

Dewey smiled. "I doubt it. But who knows what causes earthquakes, right? This IS Los Angeles. Whole lotta shaking going on."

"And you think the army hasn't noticed you have one of their warheads?"

"They've lost track of dozens. In China and Africa. One more won't make much of a difference. Besides, plenty of people in the government know who I am and what I intend to do. They've been surveilling me for months, but they've done nothing. The spies are hoping for an increase in their budgets. Most of those bureaucrats in Washington and Chicago can't stand California anyway. Tell them Los Angeles is going to fall into the ocean and they'd applaud."

"The man was clearly insane. He wanted to kill them all. The Baby Boomers. The Generation Xers. Hated them worse than lepers. He wanted to kill them in their cars."

Los Angeles. The mid-2020's. Rock MacLean is an A-list actor at the height of his fame…handsome and wealthy. But middle age is creeping up. With nowhere to go but down, his wife is threatening to leave him and take their two little girls. No wonder—even Rock thinks he might be a sex addict. Far from having it all, Rock's about to lose everything. And he doesn't even care.

But when a drug deal with Nicaraguan gangsters goes sour, Rock finds himself in the path of Dewey Lane—a fanatical army colonel with a plan to wipe Southern California off the map. Trapped in a mountainside bunker, Rock watches helplessly as Dewey sets off an electronic pulse—causing the simultaneous destruction of every automobile in Los Angeles.

But that's only phase one of Dewey's plan. Phase two? Nuclear Armageddon. And only Rock can stop it. 1980 "The Year the Past Disappeared" is a novel where delusion, sex, and cheap weapons of mass terror intersect in a satirical look at a materialistic and cynical future.

IN THE

MID-2020'S,

EVERYTHING
CAME INTO
FOCUS...

1

It had been far too long since Rock MacLean had reapplied his sunscreen. The bright California sun streamed down. Never in his life had he been more in need of an umbrella. And soon.

Next to him a Japanese soldier bent down. Placed a large ceramic bowl on the ground. Pushed it in his direction. Liquid slopping over the sides, turning the dirt to mud. Rock lifted it to his lap and looked at the contents derisively. His brown military uniform turned dark as the soup spilled over the edge of the bowl. It looked like he goddamn well pissed himself.

"What the hell is this?" he asked the soldier.

"Breakfast ramen. For the prisoner."

"You think I'm going to eat your Commie food?"

"Do you prefer to starve, American?"

Rock met the man's gaze. He took the bowl with one

hand and fired it as far as he could. "I don't need your noodles. And I don't need your attitude. For the last time, you're making a big mistake."

"The only mistake," said the soldier in thickly accented English, "is you, Yankee."

KA-BOOM!

Over the far hill, a line of bombs detonated. An entire cavalry of soldiers, dressed identically to Rock, streamed over the ridge on horseback. Each firing guns in the direction of the prison camp. All around Rock chaos erupted. He stood up and beckoned to a line of prisoners behind him. Leading them to escape the compound. The Japanese soldiers who would usually hold them back were now totally distracted.

The soldier that had passed the bowl to Rock screamed orders at his subordinates in Japanese. Rock figured he must be from California. He was using vocabulary that went out of common usage a hundred years ago. As Rock and his compatriots scampered around, explosions went off in the dirt all around them.

Each of the cavalry raised their bayonets high, exposing their Nazi swastika armbands. They're perfectly round, like targets, thought Rock as he crouched down. Fighting a line of soldiers, the last of which carried the flag of the Japanese Empire. A bit over the top, he thought. What soldier sees an invasion force and immediately grabs a flag?

Rock, like the rest of the prisoners, wore the uniform of the SS. It had been modified to cope with the arid conditions of Southern California. But it was still hot. Rock was thankful he wasn't on horseback.

4

With the prisoners, he reached the far perimeter fence. With one massive combined motion they pushed on the chain link barrier. Collapsing it. Rock held still as a line of Nazis rode past. More explosions followed. In the distance, gunfire. An explosion went off a bit too close to him. What had he been thinking doing this without earplugs? Permanent damage wasn't worth the paycheck.

The smoke got thicker. Not good. He couldn't see anywhere. But he still heard the horses galloping. Someone could get trampled.

BOOM!

That explosion was way too close.

A Nazi soldier fell at his feet. Made sense. Face all bloodied. They did a pretty good job on him, he thought. Rock looked around. The smoke wasn't clearing. That only meant one thing.

From the bullhorn: "Okay, everybody. Cut! That's a cut!"

Rock stood still as the commotion calmed down. The smoke was shut off. The sightline between him and the A-camera cleared. Did they get any of this?

Rock turned around and faced the enormous green-screen. The only thing separating the studio backlot from the residential streets of the San Fernando Valley.

He looked over to the tent where the first assistant director was shouting orders into his Comdex mike. "Where's my goddamn umbrella?"

A young man from the makeup department ran over and raised a white parasol. "Here you go, sir."

"Thanks, what's your name? Andy?"

"It's Andrei."

"Like Tarkovsky?"

"Yeah. Exactly."

"Great. This scene is a fucking mess. Did you watch it on the monitor?"

"Only the A and B-cameras. There was a lot of smoke."

"Seven cameras. And we'll never get it done properly after the reset. Why doesn't Simpson just take a suitcase full of hundred dollar bills, and light them on fire? It would cost half as much and be twice as entertaining."

The fog of the fake movie smoke was finally dispersing. They had hired a dozen smoke guys, each dressed like auto mechanics. Which was about ten too many.

Rock looked up at the giant greenscreen. It was awfully close to him. The parasol looked green. Someday, many months from now, it would be the ruined, post-apocalyptic city of Los Angeles. If the Director of Photography hadn't fucked things up. The guy was doing his first big budget feature, and Rock worried they were shooting it like a ten-dollar documentary. Whatever. Not his department.

Rock turned to the mass of people crowded around the A-camera. "Simpson? Where's Jennifer?" She was the makeup girl who took care of Rock. "This is going to take a whole fucking hour to reset. I'm sweating my balls off out here. No one told me there was going to be fifty people on horseback." This was one of Simpson's usual tricks. He thought he was doing cinema verité.

Andrei looked over. "He wanted to get a reaction from you. Of surprise."

"No shit. And who's going to see it through all that smoke? If you ever become a director, Andrei, it never hurts to tell the actors what to do. Just so they don't get run over by the cavalry."

Rock looked down. The stuntmen were waiting for the order to reset from the 1st AD. Two of them got up. Neither had blood or gore makeup on their faces. That was weird, he thought. "Good job, guys, thank you so much," he said as they sauntered past.

"Hey, listen," said the first Nazi, "we do it for kicks." He looked at Andrei. "Don't work for Hitler when you grow up."

Andrei nodded. "Sure thing."

Rock looked down at the stuntman at his feet. The one who landed hard after the explosion. "That's quite the makeup job on your face. How long did that take this morning?"

The man just lay there. Rock noticed blood pooling around his neck. Pulsing out of a gash near a piece of shrapnel. Rock leaned down and shook the guy. "I think they're resetting. Maybe you want to get back in the shade."

Still no response. Rock stood up and looked toward the crew, still crowded around the monitors, watching the replay. He turned to Andrei. "Can you call the medics?"

"I don't have a Comdex. Sorry."

"Simpson!" screamed Rock towards the crew.

"Simpson!" He saw the director sneaking away, probably back to his air-conditioned trailer.

1980 "The Year The Past Disappeared"

Rock bent back down to the stuntman. "Hey man, get up. They're not rolling any time soon." Rock poked at the gash. It felt warm. His hand was covered with blood. The stunt man wasn't breathing. He smelled his fingers.

The blood was real.

The stuntman was dead.

2

Cochese Murray was having a really bad day. As the first assistant director, or 1st AD, he was the main person in control of the set. One of his main responsibilities was the safety of the cast and crew.

Which was why Rock was screaming at him.

"What the hell? That man is dead. Where the hell did shrapnel come from? Have you even tested these effects?"

"We're looking into it right now."

"There's nothing you can do. I've got that guy's fucking blood on my hands."

Cochese was escorting Rock back to his trailer on the other side of the studio lot. Usually the transport guys would have a car ready to go. But Rock had refused.

"It looks," said Cochese, "like one of the explosions went off too close to the wire fence. It must have blown it apart, flinging shrapnel into the stuntman's throat."

"Is he going to live?"

"No."

At that exact moment an ambulance flew past them, heading across the parking lot. Sirens blaring.

Rock stopped and turned around, his eyes following it.

"Just a minute—" yelled Cochese.

"Don't fucking minute me. I could've been the one killed out there. And you wouldn't have a movie." Rock stopped and grabbed Cochese by his T-shirt. Smearing blood all over the light brown material. "Don't push me right now." It took a moment before he realized Cochese was shaking in fear. He let go. "Look, I'm sure this isn't your fault. But it's what you get when the son of a second-rate comedian directs an action picture. He doesn't give a shit about safety. Or even getting the scene. It's all about his ego."

Rock turned back to his trailer and started walking. The journey continued in silence. Until he saw someone sitting on the back steps of a cube truck, his head buried in his hands. It was the special effects guy. The man in charge of the explosion.

"Hey, you—over there—"

The man looked up. He'd been crying. "I don't know what went wrong. There was an explosion—"

"Are you out of your mind?" Rock yelled.

The guy pretended to hear something on his comdex. "Look, I have to go back to set. We have to run a bunch of checks to find out what went wrong."

"We better be shutting down for the day."

"I don't know," said Cochese.

10

Rock sneered. "Well, we better shut down. Or I'll shut YOU down."

A young blond woman ran up. Sandra, the actor's union rep. "Rock, we're taking photos of everything right now—oh, my God—"

Rock looked down at his hands. She was freaked out by the blood. Her reaction made him realize something. She was the first person he'd talked to since the accident who wasn't completely high on cocaine.

"This is unbelievable," she said. "And we've got all these guns..."

Rock turned to Cochese. "Some of those were pointed at me. Did you even check them? How about the fence? It's not like we're out in the middle of the desert here. This is a studio backlot."

"I'm trying to maintain order," said Cochese. "I need to get back to set..."

"Do you know what the press is going to say about this? They're going to talk about my name in connection with the death of a crewmember. And those lazy creeps will probably bungle the story so bad that I'll look like a homicidal maniac by the end of it." Rock turned to Sandra. "I'm not doing anything more on this picture until you check every single one of those weapons, okay? And I'm not doing anything while there's explosions on the set."

Cochese looked at him. "Sir, you must understand, the number of horses and people we're paying for—"

"Back off, buddy," came a voice from the other side of the trailer. It was Simpson Shore. The director.

11

He appeared right in front of Rock. "My staff is doing their best to get to the bottom of this. It was a terrible accident. But that's all it was. An accident. We brought in the double for that stuntman and we'll continue once the horses are reset."

Rock stared at him, incredulously. "You're out of your fucking mind."

Simpson shook his head. "Every fifteen minutes we're burning the average retail price of a luxury German automobile. The cost of your walk over here could buy me a new Harley. Once we've got this sorted out, we'll continue."

Rock couldn't believe the arrogance. "You don't know what the fuck you're doing. There's a lineup of 34-year-olds behind that studio gate, ready to take your job. There are people directing cough syrup commercials that could do what you do. Without killing people."

"That is such an actorish thing—"

"I'm going to fucking kill him." Rock lunged.

Simpson's scrawny figure was no match for Rock's six-foot-two frame. And Rock had been working out at a gym on Venice Beach for months. He got in a couple of shots to Simpson's face before Cochese and Sandra pulled him off.

"I'm going to kill you," said Rock, "and there'll be two bodies to carry away from set." He looked over at Sandra. "What are you staring at? Go back to your chair by the craft truck. Loading up on Skittles." Rock looked over and saw the continuity person, Samantha, approaching.

"Rock," said Samantha. "Calm the fuck down. It's not his fault, okay? Somebody has died. These people are working to prevent it from happening again. We are going to finish this scene. Unless you're prepared to put your career on the line to shut us down."

He looked her over. She was a knockout. But she had bigger balls than most men he knew. Figuratively, of course. She was also the only person on this shoot who could handle him.

Everyone was sweating. The parking lot was sweltering. Simpson wiped the blood off his face.

Rock turned to Samantha. "I'm going back to my trailer. Join me when you have a moment."

"Sure," she said.

Rock walked away to clean himself off.

3

After five minutes keeping Rock on hold, Ira finally picked up the phone. "What can I do you, Mr. MacKenzie? My favorite client. It's going to be a tragedy when I'm forced to leave, isn't it?"

Rock let a silence hang in the air before he began speaking. "Do you know what happened today?"

"No, tell me." Ira was used to taking Rock's irate phone calls. No tone of voice could waver his casual, relaxed manner. Ira had been Rock's agent for the last twelve years. He was a Jew. Rock's favorite Jew. In a business filled with Jews. Typically Rock thought of his co-workers without consideration of their cultural background. But Ira seemed to enjoy reminding Rock that he was Jewish. Reporting his various concerns and delights about it. Nary a conversation went by where Ira hesitated to point out that he was, in fact, a Jew. And he never held back his opinions on Israel, the Orthodox Jewry, or any other matters concerning his cultural baggage, to the point where Rock seriously wondered if one day there might be a quiz on said topics. As it was his wont, Ira had no problem announcing his latest bout of perceived anti-Semitism. In fact, he complained so often that Rock wondered if Ira even took it seriously himself. Rock suspected not. The guy had no problem procuring him a role as an American neo-Nazi officer. The payday was too good to pass up. "Whatever it is, I'll have it taken care of. You just need to relax."

"You don't understand. Somebody's dead."

"What? Have you phoned the police? Don't. I'm heading right—"

"Not someone I killed. It was a stuntman."

"What? A crew member?" Rock could hear Ira sitting back down in his chair. "You mean, on set? You should talk to the first AD. He's in charge of safety."

Rock outlined the events of the morning. "I could be dead right now, you know. It was one of those retarded new special effects things. You know, the ones that produce the different color smoke? Made of cobalt, or something."

"Look," said Ira, losing patience, "I'll come down there and talk to the producer. In a few hours—"

"I want this whole thing shut down."

"Look, this isn't my department. I negotiate deals. And I'm moving out of my office this week, as you know. The person replacing me is competent in getting people work. It's going to make her job tougher if you start this diva bullshit just as she's taking over. If word gets around town, there's nothing I can do. I'm crossing over to the other side. My advice is to let these people do their jobs. Put it out of your mind. And carry on."

"But Ira—"

"The head of that production company is a valuable part of the ecosystem that sustains your career."

"What kind of bullshit is this?"

"It's not bullshit. You've been shooting for six months. Let's get this finished and move forward."

Six months, thought Rock. It had been the most difficult shoot of his career. A film adaptation of The Man in the High Castle by Phillip K. Dick. Ira, the crown prince of the Hollywood Jews, had convinced Rock to play an anti-Semitic American Nazi in an alternate future United States. Which had been divided up between different groups of competing Nazis, the Empire of Japan, and Canada. Ira seemed to like how the protagonist's arc involved him going on a crusade against racism. Rock thought it all a bit too cute. But he trusted Ira when he said the script was good. So Rock went along with it.

Also there was the fact that it was the last remaining Phillip K. Dick story never having been filmed. In the words of one press release, the most ambitious science-fiction movie ever attempted. Months spent in the tropical climate of Thailand, which had become the go-to place for runaway productions. Then off to northern Italy during the end of the worst winter in thirty years.

Today was Day 104 of 105. According to the call sheet. Rock was fed up with the whole agonizing process. Simpson had only made one movie before this. A low-budget indie shot for nothing in practically no time. But it had spent a lengthy spell in post-production. Somehow Simpson had convinced a studio head that he was the guy for the Dick job. Even though his previous film had been filmed in seventeen days. With a total budget that didn't exceed what was spent on licorice and cheese sandwiches for this production. He wasn't just in over his head, he was exhausted. Too many fifteen-hour days.

For one thing, Simpson had no idea how to direct with practical special effects. Things like explosions, rain, and smoke. Sure, the guy had worked for years in commercials. It had given him a sense of style, and the ability to work efficiently with a crew. But he knew nothing of how to tell a story. Or get good performances. He had no idea how to direct an action scene with a hundred extras on horseback. And seven cameras rolling.

Naturally, Simpson would never admit this. He refused any suggestions from more experienced people like Cochese. It was his way or the highway. Even if it was the wrong way. And now somebody had died.

Somehow, in the last forty-some years since Phillip K. Dick's death, Hollywood had managed to exploit every single one of his stories. The sheer amount of

18

money collected by the author's estate dwarfed the GDP of several African countries. Unfortunately, during his lifetime Dick had seen, well, dick of all these moneys. A life cut short by liver disease brought on by a particular period of heavy drug use in the early seventies. And the fact he consumed vast quantities of speed every time he sat down at the typewriter.

With that kind of pedigree, Rock had been willing to overlook the director's inexperience. To be honest, he actually enjoyed Simpson's first movie. It was a science-fiction alternate-world version of American history. Very similar to The Man in the High Castle. Where neither Ronald Reagan nor John F. Kennedy had been assassinated. The film was about a group of commandos who blow up the Berlin Wall, leading to the collapse of the Soviet Union. Fanciful right-wing fiction that nonetheless refused to go over the top like, say, Red Dawn, another movie of the same ilk.

This movie went back even further, to the early sixties, so it was even more of a period piece. Thailand stood in for Vietnam and Kyushu. The production had chosen to film there because it was currently the only country in Asia, besides Japan, not consumed by war. Rock's time there was pleasant and debaucherous. He wanted his life to stay that way.

Everyone was relaxed when the unit decamped to Milan. You would think it would go even smoother than Thailand, but no such luck. Every day was chaos. Tempers flared. They came back to Los Angeles to find their soundstage had been double-

19

booked. The production manager and Cochese had to rearrange the schedule in a panic so the backlot days got put to the end of the shoot. Terrifying everyone if the weather didn't co-operate. In a normal production this battle scene would have been shot two months ago. When things got dragged to the end of the schedule people got tired. And burnt out.

Everything had gone fine in the beginning. Script read-throughs, costume fittings, all that nonsense. Simpson had even left some money in the budget for a week's worth of rehearsals. Unheard of these days. But within the first ten days of shooting, Rock discovered that Simpson simply didn't understand how actors functioned. When he didn't get what he wanted, he resorted to giving line readings. Which made everyone wonder if Simpson understood the purpose of casting. All these directions only insulted Rock and the other actors. Simpson said he'd seen it in a Michael Caine video, and that was good enough for him. It wasn't like Rock had begged for this role. They had pursued HIM. Nonetheless, nothing made Simpson happy.

The malaise had lasted through the production. Things had really come to a head in the last month. Most mornings Simpson arrived terrified of making a decision. Leaving the gaffer with nothing to light. And everyone waiting around. By now, most had written the film off as a turkey, beyond saving. They just wanted to go home. With so many days of overtime, the original team of assistant directors had quit. Cochese had been brought in, but he seemed in over his head, too.

20

Cochese was in charge of the set. Coordinating where all the actors and extras are. Making sure safety rules are observed. And handling much of the paperwork—this crew seemed to at least have that under control. But everything else had taken a back seat.

"Look, Ira, something's got to be done here. The union rep doesn't give a fuck. I'm pretty sure everyone's been high since we got back from Milan."

"You've seen drug-taking on set?"

"No. But it's in their eyes."

"Listen, Rock. Two more days. Can't you hold it until then? I'll phone David in the office, but what do you want me to do? Everyone in town is convinced the thing's a piece of shit."

"Except you."

"They always say that when the rushes are screened. Trust me, things will come together by the time they put in the temp music."

"Great."

Ira was on his last week as a talent agent. Next Tuesday he started his new job heading up Universal, the studio backing this film.

"Remember, this anger inside of you? It's not about Simpson, or the movie. It's about your wife. When this is done, you need to talk to her."

4

The road that passed by Lompoc Federal Penitentiary was surprisingly bucolic. You could almost say it was beautiful. At least, that's what Major Dewey Lane thought as he sat in the driver's seat of the Chrysler Town and Country minivan. Parked across the street from the prison gates. Next to a line of deciduous trees that provided shade from the stifling California heat. Around him lay nothing but farms, the mountains rising up against the horizon. A lovely place to be. Clearly the federal government had seen its beauty and decided it could not go without being institutionalized. That was why the maximum-security prison was down the road from the air force base.

Lompoc, California has roughly eighty-five thousand people. A two-and-a-half hour drive from Los Angeles.

Out of the way on Highway 1. Few people stop by. Unless they were a die-hard surfing fanatic, and had to mark the local beach off their list. Which was on the other side of the air force base.

Today Dewey was dressed in casual clothes. His army uniform was pressed and dry cleaned, for later. He glanced at the clock on the radio. Ten-thirty. Any minute now. Maybe his presence would arouse suspicion, not driving into the main parking lot. Maybe not.

Today was release day for the Nicaraguans. The men doing his bidding. Dewey looked up from his phone. At the top of the hill they appeared. Six men, all dressed head-to-toe in denim. Shirts and jackets matching their jeans. They certainly stood out against the green backdrop.

The men knew exactly where to go. They crossed the road. Right to the minivan.

"Hey," said their leader, a tall man with dark bushy eyebrows. "You never told us you'd be parked so close."

"Get in. Hurry up. We've got to go."

They piled into the back as Dewey started the ancient hybrid engine. The vehicle was at least twelve years old. He turned onto the main road and headed back into town. Very likely they were being monitored by some automated algorithm. Designed to track recent parolees. Fortunately for them, it was only able to track clothing, which was why Dewey had insisted the Nicaraguans dress only in single-color denim. While it made the algorithm's job easier, it also made the surveillance easier to avoid. Switching out of the denim was stage one.

They headed into town. Down the main street of Lompoc. Hitting all major surveillance camera positions. Then Dewey headed up to the Mission Hills neighborhood. An area dotted with upper-middle class family dwellings. Lompoc's city planning screamed mid-twentieth century suburb. Every store in the downtown had ample parking. Mission Hills homes had ample yards, plenty of space for people to mind their own business. Sometimes.

The Chrysler pulled up to a sprawling white rancher. Dewey hit the remote garage door opener and backed in. When the door headed down, they all got out.

"Okay," he said, "any of you hungry?"

No one nodded.

"If you have to shower or head to the restroom, do it now. It's going to be a long day. I suggest all of us eat."

"I don't think I'll be hungry for another couple hours," said the man with bushy eyebrows.

"Well, now's the time."

They headed into the kitchen where Dewey had prepared a meal of burritos and rice. Then the men cleaned themselves up and changed into standard issue military fatigues. All were dressed as grunts—all privates, except bushy eyebrows, who got the warrant officer's uniform. Dewey had changed into his regular clothes, as a Major. Right now most of the American military thought he was on leave.

He handed each of the Nicaraguans an ID badge.

25

"These are in your own names. Be very careful. Show them if anyone asks for them, okay?"

The men nodded.

Dewey grabbed a wooden crate lying next to the kitchen counter. Flipped open the lid to reveal a cache of M-16 assault rifles. With plenty of ammo. Each man was given a gun and a generous supply of bullets.

"These aren't loaded. Be very careful once the magazines are in."

Once they had their guns, Dewey gave them a brief tutorial on how they would be expected to hold their weapons. Three of them had been in the army before. The other three required more work.

They headed back to the garage. Next to the minivan was a Mercedes station wagon. They stored their guns in the back and piled in. Headed out to a warehouse at the edge of town. Where the industrial area gave over to sage brush.

In the warehouse they changed vehicles again. To a military M35 transport with a green canvas roof. The transformation was complete. Dewey took the wheel, bushy eyebrows riding shotgun. Everyone else in the back. They drove to the air force base.

The M35 pulled up to the front gate. Dewey flashed his ID at the automated scanner. The device briefly beamed its laser into his eye. He passed the computer's inspection. The metal road spikes lowered, the robot machine guns pointed skyward, and the red stoplight turned green. Everything was going perfectly. Such a brilliant idea getting rid of the guard manning the front gates. Saved the federal government millions in liabilities. For someone in Dewey's position, there was no way they could stop him. An ordinary soldier might have gotten suspicious. Checked the back. But it would take them a week before they'd get around to discover why Dewey had entered the base.

He drove the truck to an out of the way barracks not currently in use. Dewey backed the truck up to the door. The Nicaraguans got out of the back. Dewey produced a set of keys that unlocked the entrance to the makeshift building. It was basic. And mostly empty. A spare facility if the military needed to house people in a hurry. They quickly unloaded equipment from the back of the truck into the main room of the building. The sleeping quarters.

"Now," said Dewey, "all of you must be careful. Open that box, the grey one."

Most of their cargo was painted army green. Except one box, painted blue. Inside this particular blue box was a round metal thing, which came apart like a Russian egg. In the center was a cube lined with tubes and wires.

"What you see there is an exact metal replica of the nuclear device."

Dewey motioned to bushy eyebrows, who picked up an instrument with a digital display. Attached to it was what looked like a microphone.

"That is a Geiger counter. Right now, what does it say?"

"Zero-point-zero-zero," said bushy eyebrows.

"Exactly. When we do this, those numbers might get pretty high. If the alarm rings, we're in real trouble. That's why we have to be careful. Okay? The rest of the day will be spent practicing on that model. Taking it apart, and putting it back together. Each of you will do it one hundred times."

One of the men scoffed. "Why do we got to do that?"

"Because," said Dewey, "it will give you something to occupy your time until tonight. I don't want you to get bored. By then, hopefully, dismantling the device will become second nature to you. Safety first, as they say."

The men nodded.

"Once night falls, we will begin the operation."

5

The guy's name was Louie Liu. The one-man revival of the Hong Kong action star in the tradition of Jackie Chan and Chow-Yun Fat. For the first time since the turn of the century. He was tall, handsome, and muscular.

And he was hitting on Vivian Zhang, the morning traffic reporter for KXXX news. Louie was doing his best to chat with her in Cantonese. She didn't have the heart to tell him her parents were from Taiwan, and she barely caught a word of what he was saying.

Vivian was pretty sure he was trying to describe his latest film role to her. His first in a major Hollywood production. Which she had absolutely zero interest in.

Finally Louie switched to English. He gazed into her eyes. "I think you're absolutely beautiful."

1980 "The Year The Past Disappeared"

Vivian glanced around the makeup room awkwardly. Where was the rest of the staff? To be fair, she was surprised—men didn't usually say that to her. Never, in fact. Personally she felt she was rather plain looking. "Why, thank you." She felt up his arm. Muscular. "You're not so bad yourself."

"When you're done today... why don't you come visit me in my hotel room? For lunch, of course."

"I would love to, Louie. But you know I'm married." She raised her hand, showing off her wedding ring.

Louie rolled his eyes and backed off. He clearly wasn't used to American women and their sense of fidelity. Or maybe he wasn't used to any woman having a sense of fidelity. Around him.

To Vivian, he was just another actor in Los Angeles. He might have been famous, but he wasn't THAT famous.

RUFF-RUFF!

She looked down and saw Finnegan pressed against the front of his cage. Barking could only mean one thing. Vivian grabbed the baby milk bottle from a nearby counter. Opened his cage and fed him. "There you go."

Louie petted the dog's bright orange fur. "This is an Akita dog, right?"

"Yes," said Vivian, scooping him up into her arms. "Isn't he beautiful? He came all the way from Japan."

Finnegan let the plastic nipple go. "All done." She turned to Louie. "You'll excuse me, we have to go on the air in a minute."

30

"He goes on camera with you?"

"Yup. Keeps the viewers entertained when there isn't a major accident."

"How do you keep the dog so calm under the bright lights? Doesn't he bark?"

"Well...um... I add a little bit of bourbon to his milk. Keeps him calm."

Vivian said her goodbyes and headed down the long hallway to the studio, Finnegan in her arms. To a set of large blue doors. The red light was dark. Still on commercial.

She yawned as she sat down at the anchor desk. Glanced at the clock on the studio wall. A quarter after four in the morning. Louie must still be on Hong Kong time. No problem sneaking in an interview before his call time. Vivian had never gotten used to the hours of a morning news shift. Some nights she awoke in terror that she had overslept. Even though she lived only a twenty-minute drive to the studio.

It helped that her husband, Doug, was the entertainment reporter. Who also pulled the early shifts. Finnegan leaned on the desk as she checked for Sig Alerts. Nothing yet. At four a.m. the highways were mostly clear. But by five or six things got rough. All the new subways had made Los Angeles a more, not less, dangerous place to drive.

After commercial things went smoothly. Finnegan behaved. Of course, at this hour the only people awake were film workers, stoned college students, and the mentally ill.

1980 "The Year The Past Disappeared"

It wasn't until half-past when things went off the rails. Doug, her husband, had slipped in during the weather report. Between the two of them, he wasn't the brains in the relationship. Still, he was blond and tall and handsome in a bland kind of way, and he stuck to entertainment journalism. Most of his job consisted of using the cut and paste commands on a word processor.

He was interviewing Louie at a desk across the studio when she heard him call the Hong Kong actor Lawrence. With growing horror she realized Doug had mistaken Louie for another Chinese actor, Lawrence Lee. The grandnephew of Bruce Lee.

"So," said Doug, "it must be wonderful to be carrying on the family tradition."

Louie smiled. "It's a bit early in the morning, I guess I didn't quite catch your question."

"Well," Doug said, "you granduncle was quite the institution."

"He ran a bakery in Macao."

Doug went red with embarrassment. Louie caught on, and reminded him that he wasn't related to the noted martial arts star of the 1970's. "But," he said, "I'm sure to you, all us Chinese people look the same."

"Um…ah…"

"How about I tell you about my latest film?"

Vivian rolled her eyes. And leaned in to Finnegan. "What do you think? Should I divorce your Daddy?"

6

Rock was a floating wave of consciousness in the grey ether. But that wasn't quite right. Grey implied a color. Which implied something was there. But there was nothing. No color. Grey was just the best way of describing it.

His heart.

He felt it beating. He was returning back from the nothingness. He would be sad to see it go.

Waves and waves.

An ocean of purgatory.

This is what death feels like.

An endless grey wall that never bounds you in.

The room came back. Rock was in his trailer. In the seat, where the makeup department came to fix him up.

In front of him he saw Andrei. The production assistant. Looking at him. Worried.

"Ahhh...eeiii...yahh?"

Andrei moved in closer. "Maybe I should call an ambulance."

Rock looked over at the pipe resting on the side table. Good. At least he'd managed to set it down before his consciousness had begun to dissociate. The white powder was burnt. His mouth had that old familiar chemical taste. Not quite real. But not quite artificial, either.

Andrei reached up and felt Rock's forehead. "What is it? What did you do?"

Oh, Rock leaned back as a grin spread across his face. Happily. He couldn't stop smiling if he wanted to. "I just smoked a bunch of DMT."

"What?"

"Actually, it was 5-MEO-DMT. It's the wildest shit. I've seen death. There's nothing waiting for us."

"You were screaming."

Rock looked over. The record player had stopped. Timesteps by Wendy Carlos. The music had gotten to the end and entered an endless loop. Rock reached over and switched it off. "What can I do for you?"

Andrei handed him some paper. "These are the new sides."

"Oh...god... they rewrote it again?"

"They're almost ready to shoot."

"But I haven't had time to memorize it. And do my homework on them."

Andrei grimaced. "I just deliver it."

Rock looked over the goldenrod sheets of paper.

There was no way his brain, in its current state, could ever hope to memorize anything. Usually after a DMT trip he was useless for at least an hour. They'd already done a scene this morning. The gaffer hadn't been optimistic they'd get the next setup ready before lunch. They had to set up horses and smoke effects. What happened?

Fifteen minutes later Rock groggily rolled up on set.

"Okay, so," said Simpson, "in this scene you're to befriend the Japanese colonel. Explain you're the right man to join forces with him."

"Huh?"

The Japanese soldier was being played by some Hong Kong actor who Rock hadn't seen since the Thai shoot. And then only briefly. They shook hands. "You're Lawrence, right?"

"Louie. Louie Liu."

"Right, sorry. I saw your interview this morning. That was terrible. That doughhead interviewed me last year. He thought I was from England."

"You're not American?"

Rock laughed. "No. Canada. From Cape Breton. On the east coast. Closer to England than here, I suppose."

They ran through the scene while the crew watched. They got halfway through before Simpson called cut. "What are you doing, Rock?"

"Back off, let's just do it again."

Did he have to yell at him in front of the crew? It was so embarrassing.

They ran the scene again. This time his mind went blank. So he made up lines from what Louie was saying.

"Cut! Rock, we have to get this. Why don't you know your lines?"

"Well, how about you just shout them to me and I'll repeat. Cause, I can't memorize this shit in fifteen minutes. Or give me a comdex in the ear or something."

Simpson exploded. "Why don't you know this scene? It's your job. It's called acting."

Rock just stared blankly as Simpson continued babbling and berating. Finally he paused his string of complaints. He turned to Cochese. "Here's what we're going to do. Get out the cue cards."

Simpson turned to Rock. "No wonder you've got nothing lined up after this."

7

They made love furiously. In the back of Rock's trailer. Samantha, the continuity girl, had walked in to find Rock in his bathrobe. A signal that he wasn't looking for an appetizer from the caterer. She had immediately closed the door. Locked it behind her. Stripped her clothing off. Without a word, she straddled him with her long legs, pushing her ample chest into his face.

It took Rock less than thirty seconds to ejaculate inside of her. He couldn't bear her body any longer. Samantha was delighted to see him so excited. With a satisfied face she leaned down towards him and cuddled.

A regular lunchtime quickie. One of the few good things this job had provided him with.

Rock looked up at the clock. Two-fifteen. They had forty-five minutes. One of the craft service people knew about their relationship. Rock slipped him a hundred-dollar bill every now and again to discreetly send two trays of food to his trailer. Just before lunch was called. After all, the guy was probably earning minimum wage.

She kissed his throat. He felt down her vagina. As his hand moved over her labia, he found her clitoris, brushing it feather-light over and over. She moaned softly, flexing her muscles. He never believed she could orgasm with so light a touch. But she always directed his hand the same way. Lighter.

Rock grabbed a tissue. His fingers were coated with come.

Samantha noticed his predicament. "God... did you have to shoot it inside of me?"

"Why? What's wrong? You're not going to get pregnant, are you?" From a very early stage, Rock had outlined the terms of their relationship. "I told you I have a wife and—"

"No, relax," she said. "It's just that I don't want to spend the rest of the day dripping your man juice all over the set. I'm wearing Daisy Dukes, you know. It's hot out there."

"Is this why all women prefer to have sex at night?"

"Basically."

"I don't have any tampons. What should we do?"

"I'll be fine." She grabbed a towel from the night-stand and put it between her legs before moving back to Rock's arms.

"So when does your boyfriend get back from tour?"

"I don't know. The Juan MacLean just added seven more dates in Europe. Could be a couple weeks after we're wrapped."

"Yeah?"

"He hasn't called me back yet. Maybe he's still waiting for a call from Bandworld."

"You're cool with that? Never seeing him all the time?"

"It's fine. He isn't the first roadie I've dated. But he always shows up without warning. He never tells me when his tour is over. Like he wants to catch me in the act. Or something. I don't think he trusts me. For all I know, he's fucking some DFA groupie or something."

"Well, you ARE cheating on him."

"Not really. This isn't serious."

"So you promise you don't love me?"

She smiled and cuddled up against him. "Promise."

"Do you love your boyfriend?"

"I don't know. He gets so moody sometimes. And I never planned to settle down with a roadie. That would be like... marrying an actor."

"How old are you now?"

"Thirty-four."

"Well, you've got plenty of time. Unless you want kids. Then you should panic."

Rock got up, went to the washroom. When he got back, Samantha was putting on her clothing. "Can you, uh, help me get into my costume?"

"Sure. You're going to have to go back through makeup." Samantha examined her face in the mirror, wiping it with a wet facecloth. "You got that dust all over me."

"Next time I won't kiss."

She continued wiping her face. "I'm thinking of joining him in Europe."

"Where are they headed?"

"Spain and Greece. And Italy."

"That sounds fun." Rock grabbed a tray and sat down at the table. "Spaniards like to kick up a good show."

She turned around, indicating for Rock to stand up. She adjusted his Nazi armband. "They're also playing in France, though."

"I thought they didn't let people in, like, you know..."

"They make an exception for entertainers." Samantha's half-black, half-Asian looks weren't going to cut it with French customs. "And their families. They just don't like us immigrating there. I suppose it makes sense. All those Algerians that came in after the African war. In the banlieues."

"You may think racism is okay, but I don't."

"This movie will play well over there. They love Americana stuff." She finished adjusting his collar and they both sat down to a lunch of salmon and salad.

Rock picked at his spinach. "I'll be happy to go back to eating pizza when this is all over."

"They've got you on a diet?"

"I didn't get this thin on my own."

Samantha gazed into his eyes. "That's what happens when you get married. You get fat."

40

He gazed at her long and hard. "I might want to leave my wife. I don't think I can handle her anymore. Maybe move down here permanently. Give up my Canadian life."

"Canada's a nice country. But it's cold."

Rocked nibbled on some salmon. "There might not be anything left of it after next month."

"Oh, yeah. I read about that in the newspaper."

"Who knows? There might not be anything left of the States the way it's going."

"Nationalism's not exactly... in... right now, is it?" she said, taking a bite of salmon.

"If I got divorced, I can't get married again. My kids would never forgive me."

Samantha's fork clanged against her plate as she stood up. A scowl crossing her face. Ignoring Rock, she headed to the door. Halfway out, she turned back to him. "You're nothing but a Mexican in a fucking sweater, aren't you?"

Rock sat there. Dumbfounded by her sudden rage.

8

Darkness had fallen. But Dewey had yet to make his move. He kept the Nicaraguans in the hangar until well after nine. He walked over and opened the door to the outside, waving in the moonlight. They piled into the back and drove to the building half a mile across the base, taking a route on the perimeter to avoid traffic.

They arrived at a non-descript hangar. Smaller and isolated from the rest of the base. Two guards stood watch by the door. Dewey parked far enough away to be inconspicuous. He took out his binoculars and watched while the shift changed. To maximize the time between the assault and when the bodies were discovered.

They drove the truck up to the door. Dewey got out and approached the guards. They saluted upon seeing his uniform.

"At ease, gentlemen. You are Corporal Leonard, and Private Gomez?" Dewey got their names from a duty roster he had downloaded.

"Yes, major," said the corporal.

"I need some help with this delivery here."

"At this hour, I don't think there's anything we can do for you. This is a restricted area."

"I understand." Dewey kept the conversation going as the six Nicaraguans snuck up behind the soldiers. Bushy mustache and one of his men subdued them both with a rear strangle takedown, snapping both their necks in the process.

Dewey nodded and took out a keychain. The hangar door had an old style metal bolt lock. Guaranteed to work if all the power was cut. He got the door open, and the group swarmed into the dark interior of the hangar. Dewey motioned for them to move slowly, just put down the bodies, and be quiet. He took out a micro-flashlight, shining its beam over the crates stored in the area.

One of the Nicaraguans moved to the wall. "Keep those lights off. Get the lamp from the truck."

Bushy mustache reappeared moments later with a battery-powered 400-watt hyper-beam light. Dewey had found the container he was looking for. He pulled a piece of paper from his pocket. Entered a ten-digit code into the container's keypad. One man switched the spotlight on. Another held the Geiger counter in the air.

As Dewey took the metal device apart the Geiger readout went nuts. But the alarm didn't go off.

Dewey looked back at the Nicaraguans and smiled.

9

Sitting in the passenger seat of the M35, Dewey looked out at the Mojave Desert as the sun crept over the mountains. They drove south on Route 14, towards Lancaster. Quite a sight. All night they had driven through back roads. Passed through Bakersfield in the dead of night. Then headed off-road to evade the surveillance cameras. In a couple of hours the military would be on high alert. They would find the vehicle, but too late to do any good. Once onto the sagebrush, Dewey had replaced the license plates. No one would track down the vehicle until it was too late.

Dewey wondered if this area had ever been a nuclear test sight. He thought about all the bombs that had been dropped none too far from here in Nevada. The locals had no idea. Even John Wayne had been out of the loop. When he made that Genghis Khan biopic. Filming for forty days on the Nevada-Utah border. Nobody knew, least of all the producer, Howard Hughes. Maybe that was what drove him to become a recluse. Sequestered for half a lifetime in the penthouse suite of a luxury Las Vegas hotel. The guilt of exposing his cast and crew to the radioactive wind. For a movie that turned out a turkey. Half of them had died of cancer by the early eighties. John Wayne himself croaked in 1979. But what does that say, anyway? Being downwind from radioactive toxicity might knock years off your life, but they weren't the good years. Does that make nuclear fallout safe, because it takes thirty years to kill you? Or dangerous, because it's going to get you either way?

Dewey figured all human beings died of cancer due to the gradual exposure to natural background radiation. Until they found a way to immunize people from plant Earth, all the cells in their bodies were doomed.

Then he thought about all the oil under Los Angeles. In the Nevada desert, there was nothing to blow up. It wasn't the radiation he wanted to unleash, it was the fire.

Oh, The Unforgettable Fire.

Under Los Angeles was an oil basin. Depleted, but still there. Still enough fuel to burn the city to the ground. With the device in the back of this truck.

The morning sun burst over the mountains, blinding him. Perhaps the city would burn for a month. Maybe even two.

They reached the outskirts of Lancaster. The desert ceded to a Wal-Mart parking lot.

"Be very careful," he told the man with bushy eyebrows. "We'll stay here until the end of rush hour. Ask the guys in the back what they want for breakfast."

10

Although Rock spoke half-decent conversational Mandarin, he had never quite gotten used to the way Chinese people addressed each other. At least when he'd been in Japan, everyone was formally referred to by their last name. You just switched it around. Mister Sakamoto became Sakamoto Mister. In China and Taiwan, they also had a tendency to avoid first names. This was all counter-intuitive to North Americans. Nonetheless, Rock had gone along with the Japanese custom. But in China, everyone seemed to be called "Little" this, or "Old" that.

Since his name was Rock MacLean, he'd be Little Rock if being addressed by his mother-in-law. But he couldn't quite get with the idea that someday he'd be called Old Rock. It sounded like a third-rate American beer.

1980 "The Year The Past Disappeared"

Rock MacLean was only his screen name. His license said David Roderick MacKenzie. But there already was another David MacKenzie in the actor's guild. That was the odd thing about Hollywood. The union wouldn't allow two people with the same screen name. Years ago, there had been an actor named Michael Douglas. Back in the seventies. Unfortunately for him, he had the same name as Kirk Douglas' son. For the rest of his career he was known as Michael Keaton. At Ira's suggestion David MacKenzie renamed himself as the bastard child of Rock Hudson and Shirley Maclaine.

His wife's name was Xi Shu. He used to call her Shu in Chinese. Or Shu Shu. Of course in English, this elicited snickers. So he suggested she pick an Anglicized name. To make things easier.

About fifteen years ago, once Rock and Shu had decided to get married, they moved back to Canada. Rock was already getting his first acting gigs. He had suggested she pick a name that was more acceptable to English ears. Shu had no problem, as most Chinese people are addressed by their nicknames outside of formal settings. The first name on his list was Tiffany. But Shu didn't like it. Most Chinese and Japanese names are based on common nouns.

So she had chosen Candy.

Rock patiently explained that it made her sound like a stripper. But Shu would have none of it. She liked its sound. And it was easy for her parents to pronounce in Mandarin. She was to become Candy MacKenzie, although most of the time she went by Candy MacLean to avoid confusion.

Rock paced around the trailer. Trying to learn his lines for yet another scene rewritten at the last minute. When he could no longer bear to go on memorizing, he made a call to his house in Canada. Candy and the children lived in Sydney, the only small city on Cape Breton Island. And the nemesis for many a European travel agent booking flights to Australia. They occupied a century-old Victorian-era dwelling. It was large and even had a separate entrance for the maid, a common feature in that era—the poor door. Both of their girls, Summer and Jasmine, had ample space to play in the front yard. And there were enough Chinese who had become locals that Candy never worried about finding the right ingredients for any dish she might want to fabricate.

Rock was feeling a bit guilty about his tryst with Samantha. He'd fallen into it easily, because, well, he didn't think anyone's feelings were on the line. But maybe he was wrong.

"Daddy! Daddy! We love you! Are you bringing us presents when you come home?"

Rock smiled. Great. "Trying to get as much out of me as possible, right?"

"Daddy's coming home soon, girls," said Candy.

"Are you getting your homework done?"

"Yes," said Summer, "and I got a hundred on a spelling test yesterday."

"Very good." Rock eyed the time on the computer. Four o'clock. That meant it was eight in the Maritimes. Almost bedtime for his girls.

Candy gave them ten more minutes on the phone, then handed them off to the nanny, a lovely old woman who came in from Main-a-Dieu every morning. When the children were gone they switched into Mandarin.

"So, you're coming back?"

"Yeah."

"You haven't been calling me."

"No, I've been busy."

"You don't want to see me? At all? While I wait here? It's five degrees today. Do you know how cold that is? Why does it take so long to get warm in this country. It's May. The weatherman says we're going to get snow tonight."

"It's been the worst winter in thirty years."

"Maybe I should move back to Taiwan. If you're never going to be around."

"You said you were happy to have some time to yourself."

"How do I know that you're not off somewhere with that lead actress—"

"Because she's twenty-four. And a dyke. I'm not her type."

"So you just stay with me because you can't attract anyone else?"

Rock smiled. "Sounds good to me," he said in English.

"AAAhhhh!" she screamed. "Why do you always treat me like crap?"

"Look," said Rock, shaking his head, "I nearly got killed yesterday." He explained the incident on set. "So even if you hate me, think about our children. If I die, someone will have to take care of my will. I'd prefer that person be you."

She calmed down after that. Candy might bitch at him, but she knew she had a pretty good deal going.

11

Rock was never all that comfortable with electronic paper. This was the year where the last newspaper in America, the Washington Post, had ceased its print edition once and for all. It had been a long time coming. He held instead what looked like regular laminated paper. But had digital ink between the layers of transparent nanofibers. It could display anything you wanted. From movies to plain text.

At least with a printed newspaper it was thick. Robust. You could find it no matter where you put it down. Digital paper was still a new thing. This sheet alone had cost Rock more than eighty dollars. Or three packs of cigarettes, as he explained to people. Someone had yet to find a way for you to log onto your web account anywhere.

The other major disadvantage was that it was flimsy. Maybe he could go into business gluing it to a more rigid material. He'd seem people in coffee shops taping their digital paper to pieces of cardboard. Making it much more comfortable to hold.

He read the headlines from Canada. The Quebec premier had announced a new Quebecois currency. In less than four weeks they had yet another referendum. To decide if they would separate from Canada and become a new nation state. This had been going on since the 1960s. For the first time, a government had asked the question directly: Do you want to form a new country, yes or no? Unlike the previous three referendums, where terms like "sovereignty-association" and "mandate to negotiate" had peppered the opaque language of the ballot.

Maron was the premier's name, and the man was serious. He would set up a barbwire border fence. Kick out all the ethnic minorities and English speakers. Establish a pure laine republic, just as France had done. English would be eliminated from all public places.

Amongst people over forty-five, it seemed like he was going to win this vote. Of course, down below on the page, another survey stated that 85 per cent of people under the age of thirty-five were preparing to emigrate. Mostly BC and Alberta, where they could put their English-language education to use. Who knows? Maybe with all the riff-raff unbelievers gone, Quebec would become an economic tiger. Unless it devolved into a white, racist version of Haiti. Rock just hoped they weren't allowed to take anything south of the Saint Lawrence. It would spoil his annual cross-country road trip.

It wasn't like Quebec was alone. Washington State had just voted to secede from the United States. Next year they were holding a referendum on whether to join Canada. Maine had just elected a secessionist party. Oregon and California were on the verge of holding their own referenda. North America might look a lot more like Europe in a few years. Or maybe Canada would just get bigger. Who knows?

Someone knocked at the door.

"Come in."

It was Ira. He was his usual jovial teddy bear self.

Rock looked up. "So, are you going to shave the beard once you become president?"

Ira smiled. "They're pushing me to. But I like the George Lucas-mountain man look." He plopped a bottle of Veuve Clicquot in front of Rock. "Compliments of United Talent. This is your last day. I didn't think you'd show for the wrap party tomorrow night."

"Simpson keeps adding scenes. There are rumors that I'll be here tomorrow. Since I have nothing lined up. You know we're re-shooting the sex scene this afternoon, right?"

"I thought you already shot that in Thailand."

"We did. But apparently the sound is all messed up."

"Can't they ADR it?"

"Apparently not. Because Mister Simpson Shore only uses tracks recorded live for his final mix."

"That's fucking bullshit. He's out of his mind."

"Simpson said he didn't do ADR on his last project, so he refused to do it now."

57

"That's because he couldn't afford the studio rental. His last movie cost five dollars."

"He's convinced that looping is responsible for the phony state of modern cinema."

"God help us if we're engaged in the process of make-believe." Ira sat down.

"Are you here to make me feel better, that I'm not dead?"

"Well, the hand-off is next week. And once I'm on the other side, the law says I'm not supposed to be offering you career advice." California had very strict laws separating the roles of agents and producers, or those who represent a production company. As the head of the studio, it was in his interest to pay all his employees the least amount possible. He'd be representing the side that tried to keep fees down for actors, writers, directors, and other below-the-line crew. However, as Rock's agent, because he could get ten per cent of the earnings, high fees were in his interest.

Of course, the grey area lay with those people called managers, who both procured jobs for the talent, took a percentage of their salary, but were also able to be producers. Which meant it was only a matter of time before a lawsuit happened. Rock didn't have management for that reason. He could read scripts by himself. Also, since Rock was bringing in so much money, Ira fulfilled the role of an old-time agent. The last of his ilk in this town. The woman taking over Rock's career managed a stable of seventy other actors. Many with a long future of earnings ahead of them.

"You know, you might think about getting a manager."

"On top of the five per cent I pay to the lawyer? And half of what's left to the government? Do you not have confidence in this person taking over your business?"

"Alexa is good. But you can't expect her to be me."

"Can't she get me some of that voice work? Where I show up in jogging pants for a couple of hours?"

"Of course. Your name carries weight in this town. But you know, things are changing. You might have to re-evaluate the audience for your films."

"You think I'm getting too old?"

"Basically. Not right now. But think ten years down the road. What will your financial position be?"

"I can't stop time." Rock adjusted his swastika armband.

"Look, a lot is riding on this film. If it goes well, I can take that to the board. You'll be a made man."

"Unless Shore sinks us."

"You might have to make due with less choice in your work. But your fee isn't going to go down anytime soon. Maybe you could Brando it."

"Almost as good as a recording booth."

Ira produced a script from his attaché case. Printed on real paper, with real ink.

Rock flipped through it. "What is this?"

"It takes place in Japan. Now, you're not in every scene..."

"I don't know..."

"You remember that movie Face/Off? With Travolta and Nicholas Cage? Same idea, except interracial."

"You just spoke my two favorite words in the English language. Who's signed to direct?"

"Randy Campbell."

"No. Absolutely not. He does cartoons."

"He did wonders with that Stretch Armstrong biopic."

"Just because we're both from the Maritimes doesn't mean we'll see eye-to-eye. He's a douche with a capital D. I met him in Tokyo twenty years ago. And he was nuts then. The guy's a fucking animator." Rock shook his head. "Find me someone with basic social skills."

"He's already signed. Promise me you'll at least read it. I can't hold you to that, but I'll tell you, it's a good script. Even if a chimpanzee was the director, you'd get an Oscar nom for it."

"That's an idea."

"As your advisor, there are two things I request of you. Save your money. And stop being successful at doing things you hate."

12

The cock sock itched. Rock had made a mistake shaving his balls three days earlier. When they filmed the scene originally, Shavon had complained about the twinges of pubic hair that seemed to sprout miraculously mid-way through the scene. Perhaps she suspected he had crabs. Or something.

Sex scenes are frequently awkward for performers. Rock considered himself lucky he'd never had to do any gay scenes, unlike several of his completely heterosexual contemporaries.

Luckily, he and Shavon got along well. They hadn't really spoken much off set. As with most professional actors, to prepare for the sex scene, they had developed a code. Each would tap on various parts of the other's body to indicate what stage of sexual excitement their character was supposed to be in. And adjust their performance accordingly. To indicate his character had penetrated her, Rock would tap the side of her thighs. She tapped below his left nipple to indicate she was giving his character fellatio. The only thing Rock had ever been told was to make it look hot. Give the audience their money's worth.

In this scene, Shavon would let Rock kiss her, then refuse to go farther. Rock would turn away, contact another girlfriend, after which Shavon would wrap her arms around him and they would begin. But rather than just re-shoot the opening in a studio, Simpson wanted to do the whole thing again.

They did a rehearsal fully clothed first. Choreographing their motions with the stunt co-ordinator. Which was weird, but necessary, since Simpson wouldn't come out from behind the video village. Then, the unnecessary crew members left the set, and they both got naked.

This didn't bother Rock. He'd never seen any of his movies. Neither had Candy. Shavon was completely naked, except for a small triangle of white between her legs. Simpson had wanted her to wear a proper merkin, something with hair and everything. But she had nixed the idea. In support of his co-star, Rock had made sure he did every scene in a cock sock, also bright white.

Later, as they wrapped their arms around each other, he couldn't stop his raging hard-on. Shavon grinned mischievously. This was terrible. He'd never had an actress encouraging him before. He focused on a spot on the bed sheets.

"And, action!"

They kissed, said their lines. Then simulated going down on each other. Shavon moaned. Much more than in Thailand. Rock tried to bury his erection between his legs, but it was doing no good.

"And, cut! Hold there. Punching in, please," screamed Simpson.

They went through the scene again. Another cut. Another take. From the start. With their clothing on. Usually directors will break up the scene for brevity. Rock looked around. They had three cameras on this.

Again they started, then stopped. But Simpson didn't come over to tell them what they were doing wrong. Finally, the stunt coordinator walked up and told them they were doing fine.

"So, when do we move on?" asked Shavon.

The makeup girl came over with a towel to shroud their bodies from the eyes of the crew.

The stunt coordinator went back to the video village, then returned, this time with precise instructions on where to place their legs.

Rock looked to Shavon. "Are they paying you extra to take your top off?"

She nodded.

"Ah... you made a deal with the devil."

"Okay," said Simpson, "going one more time. And... action!"

This continued on. And on.

"He's just getting off on this, I'll bet," he whispered into her ear as he nuzzled it.

She smiled.

"Cut! What the hell was that Rock?" He looked up and saw Simpson towering over him. "I saw you talking."

"How many more times are we going to do this? You know the movie is going to be edited once we finish shooting it, right? By an editor who knows how to select the correct takes?"

"Not if I can help it. I want this perfect. In the camera." Simpson stomped off.

That was take four. By the time they got to take twenty-five, Rock and Shavon were fed up. He'd lost his hard-on and his patience.

The stunt coordinator approached. "So, this time, he wants you to stroke the side of her breast, and the nipple."

Rock looked at Shavon, as if asking for permission.

"You can do it," she said, "but only you."

"Why doesn't he just fucking ask us himself?" said Rock, directing his voice to the boom microphone. He turned to the video village. Certain he saw Simpson sniffing something from a small bag.

Rock stood up. "I've had enough of this shit." The set had been lit with candles and a soft key light. He wanted to take one of the elaborate candleholders and shove it into Simpson's gut. Instead he ran to the director's monitor. "This is embarrassing. You have no idea what you're doing. Go, find a girl, get on that bed, and show me exactly what you want us to do."

"I'm trying to get it right," yelled Simpson. "I need your patience."

"You had it. And lost it after take twenty-four. What are you going to do? Jerk off to it in the cutting room?" Rock gripped his shirt, dragging him out of his chair.

Simpson grabbed something out of his jacket pocket. A small spray can. "Stay back! I've got mace!"

This did not stop Rock from landing a punch into Simpson's tummy. The director doubled over. Then Rock brushed Simpson's nose with an uppercut. The scrawny young man grabbed his face in agony.

Rock looked down at him writhing on the ground. Anger flooded him. He kicked Simpson's tailbone with the ball of his foot. Not with much force, but enough to elicit a howl.

Rock bent down and grabbed the can of mace. Then turned to the cinematographer. "Lazlo, you can take over while Mr. Director here recovers. For you, I'll do it one more time."

13

Rock was just about to leave for the day. As the driver pulled around to his trailer, Cochese ran up to him. "I'm really sorry about this, but we're going to need you tomorrow."

"Today was my last day."

"We only need you for the morning."

Rock checked his phone. The email with the new pages had arrived. It was just after three o'clock. "Fine."

"You only have a couple of lines. It'll be easy."

"With this director?" Rock got into the car and waved away Cochese. Then said hello to the driver. "Take me home."

"Santa Monica, right?" said the guy, who looked fresh out of college.

"Yeah. Ocean Park and Third. It'll be easiest to take the 101 to the 405."

"Sure thing, Mr. MacLean."

Rock sunk into the padded leather of the Lincoln Continental and tried to fall asleep. But a little while later he was awoken by a sudden slam of the brake. They were on the freeway. This driver obviously hadn't mastered L.A. traffic yet. He leaned forward. "So what's your name, bud?"

"It's Dougie."

"You're working in transport?"

"No, I'm an office P.A."

"Nice to meet you Dougie. So what happened to the transport guy?"

"They're full up. Some problems with the teamsters. All the protests going on today."

"What's going on? I haven't been reading the news."

"It's like a 'day of action' they're calling it. I don't know much about what they're doing. I just moved here from Iowa two weeks ago."

"It's okay, I'm from Canada. California politics are a mystery to me, too." Rock got out his cell phone. The internet was down. "Are you having trouble with your reception?"

"Oh, yeah, sorry, sir, they gave me a car with a broken dampening field."

"Excuse me?"

"It's a rental. They didn't want to get a replacement since they're wrapping tomorrow. I guess the field generator is busted. You can't get a signal in the back seat."

By law, every vehicle on the road was required to dampen all cell phone reception while in gear. A safety feature to keep drivers from getting distracted. Normally the dampening field didn't extend past the front seats. The passenger side could usually get an uninterrupted signal on their device if they held it near the armrest. But sometimes the generator overloaded and dampened the entire car. Something that was expensive to replace. Rock sighed. "They gave me the shitmobile."

"Really sorry, sir." Dougie slowed down as traffic came to a standstill. "Can I ask you a favor, sir? I have an idea for a movie."

Rock was so used to this, being a sounding board. He'd given up trying to dissuade people. "You can't copyright an idea, so don't blame me if I don't keep it a secret."

"No problem."

"You wrote something?"

"Well, not yet. But I've done an outline."

"How about you write it, then put it in a drawer. Then write five more scripts. Then take a look at the one in the drawer. After that, come back to me. You'll have a much better idea if it's good or bad."

"I get you. But it would be a big help to me, sir, if I could get your opinion, before I spend all this time and effort."

"Fine. Whatever. Can you tell it to me in five sentences or less?"

"Sure. It's really simple."

"That's two out of five. You might want to learn how to color within the lines."

"There's this guy, you see, and he's a scientist. In France. At that big collider they have there."

"The LHC? I've been there."

"Great. And he's been in an accident. Going back in time. To 1987. Where he's going to try and change the future. 'Cause his father got killed in the African War, or something. Or maybe Afghanistan. So he tries to stop it from happening."

"Okay. That's a good start."

"Except," said Dougie, "he can't convince people in the past of what's going to happen in the future. Everyone thinks he's a kook cause he tells them about automatic cars. And China plunging into civil war. And iPhones, and stuff like that."

"This all takes place in the 1980s?"

"Yeah, it'll be really cool. You'll see Michael Jackson billboards. And Max Headroom."

"That's not a bad idea," said Rock. "But you understand... it's a period piece."

"Sure, yeah, but it's, like, the 1980s..."

"Even so, it'll cost a lot of money to produce. All the costumes. The period detail. You'll have to add on days for the costume designer and makeup people to research and pick out what they need. And you'll have to rent all the old cars." Rock leaned back. "Is it mostly inside?"

"Yes. Except for the scenes set in Afghanistan."

Rock couldn't help but grin. "That's quite the travel budget."

"Well, I figure you could film it somewhere out in New Mexico."

"It's sounds great, Dougie. But I'm not sure if it's my cup of tea. Then again, somebody else might like it. Don't take that as discouragement."

"I just figured the studios need more content."

"Sure, but they'll probably take it and make it into Superman 15, or something. Or a remake of Jaws."

"But I want to see MY movie made, an original one."

Rock gazed out at the hills drifting past. "It's never been harder to get a movie made than right now. Salaries are through the roof. No one knows how to do marketing right anymore."

They passed one of the highway markers.

"Dougie, we're supposed to be headed to the 405."

"Sure thing."

"This is the 101 Southbound. Into downtown. We're going the wrong way."

"But, sir, Santa Monica is—"

"I know, but the 101 doesn't make any sense. Take the next exit and turn around."

"Jeeze, sir, I want to, but—"

Rock leaned forward. Through the windshield he saw the problem.

In the other direction, the freeway was blocked by protesters. Hundreds, maybe thousands of people marching towards them.

14

"What the hell's going on?"

"I don't know," said Dougie. He switched on the radio. "These are the people who want a referendum. Or something. They came in from Orange County. They want to separate from coastal California. Make an inland state, I guess."

Many of the marchers held signs. The closest guy, a heavily bearded man in overalls, held a placard declaring 'No tech workers! No Hollywood Jews.' All lovingly typeset around a blood-red swastika.

"I'm sure they'll be a huge market for this film we're making."

Traffic began to move again. The crowd started screaming: California for Californians. Based on the racial makeup of the crowd, "Californians" meant weathered, aging white people.

The Lincoln was approaching the exit ramp. "Get us off the highway," said Rock.

"Will do." Dougie pulled the car into the far right lane, which was still moving, slowly.

A man with a bullhorn jumped the barrier and climbed onto the back of a truck. "It's time to take this country back from the one per cent. It's time to get rid of the special interests. Let Los Angeles and San Francisco and San Diego fall into the ocean!"

The line of cars sped up slightly. "I never even seen the ocean until last week," said Dougie.

"What did you think?"

"It seems… overrated."

"I guess, if you haven't grown up around it." The car reached the halfway point on the off ramp, giving Rock a better view of the protest. "Has all the white trash in the Inland Empire shown up today? Jesus…"

"It looks mostly like people who are unemployed."

A line of protesters ran across the highway and up the grass median. They saw the Lincoln and headed right for it.

"Uh, Dougie, where are those people—"

SMASH!

Someone threw a rock against the rear driver's side window.

Dougie turned the wheel and passed a bunch of cars on the median, clipping a set of bushes as they pushed in between two trucks. The protesters stayed back.

They hit the turnoff. Dougie headed right, then left, heading the wrong direction down a one-way. "I don't think I'm cut out for Los Angeles."

Rock smiled. "A riot every now and again keeps things interesting."

"This place, it's not like Iowa." Dougie sped down the one-way street, passing through a couple of stop signs until they hit Santa Monica. "They got nice weather, but, man..."

Across the boulevard was another wall of people.

There was no way they'd get across.

15

It was a wall of Latino protesters. Dougie turned around. "I think these are the illegal immigrants. They want higher wages."

Rock looked to his left. Through the cracked glass something was happening. He slid over to get a better view. The Orange County protest had overflowed the freeway and was in the process of colliding with the Latinos. "We've got to get out of here."

"But the crowd—"

"Turn left with them and make your first right on Western."

Dougie moved in. Slowly. The protesters gave way. They reached the main intersection. At the lights Rock heard the sound of a chain saw. He thought it was a motorcycle, then a wiry middle-aged man in a bloodied wife beater appeared.

He attacked the back of the Lincoln, cutting through the bodywork. Sparks flew everywhere.

"Dougie—"

"I'm on it." He accelerated into the crowd, blaring the horn.

Rock looked back as the wife beater guy turned the chain saw on the Latinos. The crowd scattered as the street began to rain blood. Everyone ran off, down Santa Monica.

Dougie turned the car onto Western. The two marches had devolved into a rock-throwing melee. Placards swung around like weapons. The Lincoln was dinged dozens of times. They headed down Western. As the crowds thinned out, Rock sat back in his seat. He had to get out of this car. It was marked for death.

"Pull over."

"Huh?"

"Now."

The car pulled up to a deserted sidewalk, no more than half a block from the melee. Rock pulled some twenties out of his wallet and tossed them in the front seat. "I'm getting out. You get home safely." He left Dougie behind and ran. Until he found a hiding spot by a dumpster behind the Yoshinoya.

16

Rock hid until he heard sirens. There was more screaming. Gunshots. People running past. Made Rock think he should have bolted the moment he left the car. He hadn't been thinking straight after the chain saw guy.

Another twenty minutes passed. He emerged, wandering to the edge of the alleyway. It opened onto Western. And a long line of patrol cars. Maybe two dozen. Lights flashing. Bullhorns blaring. A far-off muffle directing people and traffic.

The alley branched off to a side street perpendicular to Santa Monica. He walked for about a dozen blocks. Until he hit Beverly. As the late-afternoon sun beat down on him, Rock finally felt safe from the protests.

Turning onto Western, he found an old electronics store selling used televisions. In the window were four different monitors, with four different traffic copters. Each with a different angle on the protests. It looked like most of the action was happening on the freeways. Good thing he'd left set early. None of them had reached anywhere near the water. One of the subway lines had been shut down. The Long Beach Line.

Rock looked around. He'd never been here before. It couldn't be far from the Vermont Line. Or the Wilshire Line, either. But neither would get him close to home unless he took a bus. Then he remembered the Malibu Line had just opened during the High Castle shoot. Maybe public transit wasn't so bad after all.

Rock headed south on Western. The temperature was nice. He hadn't been out for a stroll in a while. The area had a run-down, Hispanic immigrant feel, which suited Rock just fine. Lots of dollar stores, Mexican restaurants. Probably they had the best food in the city. And cheap, too. At some point this must merge into Koreatown.

Slowly Rock's thoughts drifted to his day on set. He never wanted to be put into such an awkward position again. Rock mused about the option of becoming a director himself. Instead of having someone screaming at him, he preferred to develop a sense of self-loathing on his own accord. Of course, in this town, whenever an actor announced their ambition to take the center seat, it was greeted with a collective rolling of the eyes. Sure you do. And I'm sure you'd like to be the spokesman for American Express, too.

Years ago, before he'd had any ambitions for acting, Rock used to work in the cutting room. On one TV show he'd worked on, back in Canada, he managed to wrangle a few weeks of directing duties out of the producers. He guessed they figured it kept his salary down. He certainly never got fired. Maybe his visual stylings weren't that great, but he did manage to get the best performances out of the actors. He knew how to keep people comfortable. Many directors had difficulties treating their talent like human beings. Doing simple things like saying "thank you." Especially the types that had only worked in car commercials and cartoons.

Rock checked the location on his phone. He had a tendency, while in Los Angeles, to spend his time in a bubble that stretched northeast from Santa Monica to the eastern edge of Burbank. With only occasional outings to Downtown, Huntington Beach and Big Bear. Much of Greater Los Angeles was still a mystery to him.

He was lucky if he spent three months a year of continuous time here. Rock split most of his life between Cape Breton and Vancouver. And occasionally Toronto, since Candy had a bunch of relatives there. He really didn't know L. A. as well as he thought he should.

Los Angeles wasn't the city it used to be twenty years ago. At that time it had been the second city to New York, and then only barely so, given the competition from Chicago, San Francisco, and god help us, Houston. But with all the civil wars going on in India, Pakistan, and China, Los Angeles and Tokyo had become the main centers of world power. Especially since both France and England had withdrawn from the rest of the world. New York, rather than benefiting from the lack of financial competition, had taken a serious blow. Cemented when the Dow Jones and NASDAQ headquarters moved to Hollywood, followed shortly by several major banks.

It had also been a period where things had built up. A dozen subway lines had been completed in the last five years, transforming the city. When the town had only two half-assed lines, they were seen as little more than conveyors for dumbstruck tourists and homeless people. But now the trains went places real people wanted to go. Frequently and, for the most part, on time. The ridership, almost overnight, had multiplied. Hell, even most film employees used the subway, unless they were shooting on location. The subway was connected to suburban train lines that extended the routes well into the O.C. and the Inland Empire. Which had also exported some of the homeless problem. Good for Hollywood, not so good for San Juan Capistrano.

All of this had been built with the surplus money from oil and gas royalties. Of course, the resources had been extracted from the inland rural areas, and had disproportionately benefited the urban dwellers. No small consequence of which Rock had seen in today's protests. People were beginning to be concerned that two much money was sucked away by infrastructure. California was now the leading consumer of concrete in the United States.

Los Angeles was starting to look more like Tokyo, the premier hub of Asian finance. It always had been so, but never on the scale it was now. All that Chinese manufacturing wealth, making bombs for their civil wars. And software for developed countries. The moment one dollar was made in China, it was moved to a Japanese bank account. And with the chaotic political situation in the region, there was nothing anyone could do about it. Lots of money also made it to Los Angeles. Both Japan and the United States had a policy of not asking questions as long as a Chinese name was on the bank account.

Most of China's east coast was far enough from the front line. The citizenry was unaffected by the disputed borders, running diagonally through their country. The conflict was being fought like it was 1914. Both America and Russia had a "one detonation declares war policy." If any side in the Asian civil wars used nuclear weapons, Russia and the U.S. had signed a treaty saying this meant an act of war against all nations. Thus they enabled mutually assured destruction of all countries on earth. Of course, in practical terms, the US and Russia could burn China, India, and Pakistan to a crisp on a moment's notice, since they had far more sophisticated defenses against missiles. So none of the sides in the Asian civil wars had dared go nuclear. They didn't want to face obliteration.

The Chinese were also feeding huge amounts of weapons to both the Maoists and the Democrats in India. That war had absolutely no chance of ending within Rock's lifetime. While the Chinese were fighting over ideology, the Indians were fighting over religion. With no central line. Just pockets of control by different sides all over the map. The only way to win was complete dominance over the entire sub-continent, which wasn't happening any time soon.

Amidst all this, world power had shifted to the Pacific. It seemed like most of the important people in the States had moved to Los Angeles. Creating a dense urban sprawl that was about to reach thirty million people. And kept three desalination plants running full time. Tokyo now had forty-five million, nearly half the population of Japan.

Rock fiddled with his phone. The Vermont Line connected Torrance with central Los Angeles and Burbank. But for some reason it wasn't showing up on his screen. Maybe he'd be better off walking to Wilshire. He was pretty sure it connected to the Malibu Line. The route had been named before the residents of the seaside enclave had successfully shut down their part of the project. The Malibu Line didn't actually go to Malibu. Instead it ended north of Montana, at the edge of the Palisades. And even that station only got built because of some very public lobbying by local environmentalist celebrities. Given the fears that California might be split in two, and the corresponding loss of natural resource revenue, many commentators had mused that the Malibu line would be the last underground public transit route built this century.

Rock looked at his watch. A quarter after five. The

Wilshire Line would be packed this time of day with commuters. Maybe he could hunker down in a cafe or someplace until after rush hour.

It was then that Rock noticed the neon sign glowing next to him. "Psychic masseuse" it screamed in illuminated pink. He felt his loins stirring. A remnant of the sex scene earlier that afternoon. Maybe he could get his fortune told?

Rock looked around, but the sidewalk was deserted. He opened the door and walked up the stairs.

17

The M35 lumbered up the hill, along Green Oak Drive. At the edge of the Hollywood Hills neighborhood. This was where Dewey lived. The paved road ended at a gate. Dewey grabbed a remote control from under his seat. They proceeded down a long dirt road, well obscured by foliage. The road gave way to a short concrete tunnel carved into the hillside. This lead to what appeared to be a garage door. Behind it was an area wide enough to park several vehicles, ending in a loading dock.

He turned to bushy eyebrows, who was at the wheel. "Turn us around and back us up to the gate. I'll get out and guide you."

When they were ready to unload, bushy eyebrows approached Dewey. "What is this place?"

"That's a secret. It used to be a gold mine, a hundred years ago. The government took it over during World

War Two. As a bunker. It's been in my family since they sold it in the 1980's. I've made a few renovations."

"You like living in this?"

Dewey grinned. "Let's get the device out of the truck."

He opened another door and brought out a dolly for them to move the bomb. It took all seven of them to load it off the truck. The dock led directly to a freight elevator. "How do you get so much money to keep all this up?" asked bushy eyebrows.

"I do a few flights off the clock," said Dewey. "Make sure supplies run smoothly. From South America to California. That builds up a lot of capital."

The elevator landed with a thud. Dewey reached over and lifted up the doors.

The group looked out on a wide tunnel, dug right through solid rock. It was dank and stank of sulfur. The walls were wet with humidity. Dewey reached over and flicked on an array of light switches. It revealed a tunnel that seemed to go on for miles. With a gravel floor. Not a good surface for moving the device.

Dewey and the Nicaraguans rolled and lumbered for the next three hours. It must have been almost two miles before they reached a set of train tracks. It must be how they got the old mine carts up from the bottom, thought bushy eyebrows. An old style pushcart waited for them, powered by hand.

Bushy eyebrows shook his head. "This is like something out of the 1920's."

"Help me get it onto the cart," said Dewey.

88

Together they strained to lift the device. When it was positioned to Dewey's satisfaction, he nodded, and the group made the long trudge back to the loading dock.

Back at the M35, Dewey handed bushy eyebrows the keys to an ancient Mercedes 450 parked nearby. "Your payment is in the trunk."

In the back of the Mercedes lay five large vinegar jugs. The Nicaraguans could barely contain their delight. "You are very generous," said bushy eyebrows.

"Consider it a bonus for lugging that thing through the tunnel. There's enough here to keep you and your colleagues afloat for quite some time."

Bushy eyebrows uttered commands in rapid-fire Spanish. One of the other thugs produced a bag that Dewey hadn't seen before. The man pulled out a square box with a display, attached to a long hose, at the end of which was an eyedropper. He swiveled the cap off one of the vinegar jugs and took a sample. When the readout beeped he looked over at bushy eyebrows and nodded.

"Very good, Mister Lane."

"Be careful," said Dewey, "every gangster in town will be jealous of you now."

"Well, we need to obtain some weapons."

"As a courtesy, I've left a couple of shotguns and a box of shells between the front seats." Dewey opened the passenger door and unlatched the glove compartment. "And two Glock nine millimeters. I've loaded them for you. Keep that in mind if you are stopped by police. The car is insured in your name for another year. Okay?"

"Most appreciated."

1980 "The Year The Past Disappeared"

Bushy eyebrows met Dewey at the garage exit. As the door went up, Dewey leaned in through the driver's side window. "And remember, you were never here. Got it?"

"No problem." The rest of the Nicaraguans laughed.

"And take my advice. Stay out of Southern California for the next few weeks. Your lives will be much longer if you do."

The Nicaraguans departed, taking a different route from the way they drove in. Heading through dirt back roads for a while. As they ascended the top of the mountain they turned onto the paved streets heading back down to the city through Griffith Park. As they approached the Griffith Park Tunnel, they laughed and joked with each other.

None of them spotted the Nigerian gangsters sitting at the park bench across from the tunnel entrance.

18

The flashing lights went on once they were well inside the tunnel. It seemed like a strange place to pull someone over, but bushy eyebrows stopped, not willing to take any risks.

An African-American man dressed in a police uniform emerged from the patrol car.

"License and registration, please." The man spoke in a thick foreign accent. Even bushy eyebrows, who had a terrible command of English, noticed something didn't feel right.

"What is this about?"

"One of your taillights. It's having some problems. Please stay in your vehicle." The man walked away.

Discreetly, bushy eyebrows hit the controls on the dash, flicking on the rearview camera. Both taillights were fine.

In the back, one of the men watched the patrol car. He saw someone in the rear. A man. With a gag over his mouth. "It's a trap," he yelled up front. "Drive, man, drive—"

In the backseat the men frantically loaded the shotgun. Bushy eyebrows put the car in gear. Hit the gas. No sooner had he accelerated than a black Prius appeared up ahead. It stopped. Blocked the road. Weapons emerged from its body.

A hail of bullets attacked the Mercedes.

Bushy eyebrows stopped the car. He ducked down as three of his men began firing into the Prius. The shotguns blasted it to shit.

It was over in less than a minute. The Prius had run out of ammo. Bushy eyebrows approached the Toyota. There was no one inside. The car came to life, reversed wildly, and sped out of the tunnel.

Back at the Mercedes, two of the Nicaraguans were lying in the road, dead or dying. He heard a squeal from the other end of the tunnel. The police car was speeding away. His remaining colleagues were gathered around the rear hatch.

All the vinegar jugs were gone.

19

The handjob was excellent. But at the last minute Jasmine rolled off Rock. "Turn onto your side. Come on my chest."

"Huh?"

"Come on my chest."

Rock smiled. "Okay." He complied, shooting his load all over her ample bosom. Contact with her oily skin felt good against his crotch.

Jasmine lay back, dabbling her finger in his semen.

Rock adjusted himself to make her more comfortable on the narrow massage table.

"Don't move."

Rock kept still.

She took his hand.

"What are you doing?"

"I'm a psychic. I'm reading the pattern of your ejaculate for clues to your future."

"Like other women read tarot cards?"

"Or tea leaves."

"I'm sure any girl can do that."

"No. I'm the only one here who can do it."

After a moment caressing her breasts, she lay her head against his chest, lovingly. Rock put his arm around her. She was cute, with a fantastic body. He guessed she couldn't be more than twenty years old. "So," he said, "what's my fortune?"

"You'll be fine."

"Well, I knew that."

"No, you didn't. In fact, you will have many periods where that will seem in doubt. Actually, so will I, and all the people who I've seen in the last few days." She closed her eyes and nuzzled against his chest hair. "You have a lot of complications in your life with women."

"Uh-huh. That's why I'm at a massage parlor."

"You're an actor?"

"You've seen my movies."

"Yes. Everything is changing for you, soon."

"For the worse, or for the better?"

"Yes."

"That's not an answer."

"You'll receive wisdom. You will begin to value your life again, once you have completed a series of challenges. The pleasures of your life now will cease to thrill. They'll pale in comparison to what you already have."

"All of this is ridiculously vague. I'm paying you a considerable amount of money—"

"Look, I don't give stock tips, okay? I can't tell you who's going to win the Superbowl." She leaned back into him and stroked his chest. "You play a scientist, don't you?"

"No."

"Well, you're playing a role involving science."

"No."

"Okay, but you will. Soon. Pay close attention to the script. To your lines of dialog. They may save your life."

Rock got up. "I've got to go."

Jasmine looked at him, more confident now. "Things are going to come to a head. Just be very careful."

Rock opened the door to the shower. "That's good advice at any time. In this town."

"Be careful," she said. "Something about you screams trouble."

"But you said things would work out fine."

"Yes. In the end. Not right now."

Rock left the shower door open as he washed himself off. "So you can't get a better gig? You know, working as a psychic?"

"Well," said Jasmine, joining him, "my skills are rare, even in a town like this. And my abilities don't work with women, who are the main market for most psychics."

"That's rough."

"Not too bad. I have many repeat customers. In two years, I've only had one bad client. Fortunately, after chasing me around the room, he eventually gave up and went home." She rubbed liquid soap over her body.

1980 "The Year The Past Disappeared"

"You'd be surprised how many men are worried about their future. I offer them a service that makes them feel more secure."

"Are the other girls here also psychic?"

"No. That's why they pay me extra. Unfortunately it's making them jealous."

"That's terrible." Rock stepped out of the shower and grabbed his towel. "Can I ask you one more question?"

"Sure."

"What does my future hold with my wife?"

"You shouldn't be coming here if you're married."

"She doesn't live in town."

"Whatever happens, all will work out fine. You're too cute for her to let you go."

20

Rock ended up walking all the way to the Wilshire Line. Took it all the way to Santa Monica. Along Main Street he saw no signs of protest. It was like a world away from the 101. Too wealthy for protesters, he supposed.

From the station he wandered the dozen or so blocks back to the house on 3rd Street. The digs had been provided by the production company for the duration of principle photography. The two-floor dwelling was on the east side of the road, which meant it was slightly above the house across the street, giving the front bedroom a view of the ocean. Normally people of status wanted to live right on the beach. But 3rd Street was close enough. He got less of a view, but the beach was just around the corner. And you didn't have to deal with the riff-raff.

1980 "The Year The Past Disappeared"

Two weekends ago a homeless woman, probably hopped up on meth, started a fire in one of Rock's neighbor's carports. Trying to keep warm on a night when the temperature dipped to unseasonable lows. The woman passed out after drinking a bottle of tequila. Third degree burns and a burnt down garage for the owner.

Rock mused about himself dying in a drunken binge. It had worked for William Holden, just down the street. Gashed himself halfway through the second quart of vodka. It seemed that you couldn't repair a major abdominal wound with Kleenex, so that was it for him. Think of all the press Rock would get if he died in a conflagration. Of course, the burns would be painful. Not a nice way to go out. But the idea of heading back to that set tomorrow filled him with despair.

A bit of light from the sunset remained as he arrived home. His body wanted to go to bed, but his brain felt wide-awake. He checked his cutlery drawer in the kitchen. There his worst fears were realized.

He was out of mandrakes.

Scurrying up the stairs, he burst into the room he used as a back office. He had plenty of weed and coke. A half empty bottle of umeshuu. Mushrooms, mescaline and acid. But no pills.

Fuck.

He stood perfectly still in the darkened room.

A woman's moan of pleasure cut through the night air.

The office had two windows. One looked down over the back yard. The other looked north—with a perfect view of his neighbor's garden—and her sunroom.

His body went electric.

Down below, lights were on in the sunroom. Curtains wide open. Full view.

His neighbor. Tasha. Blond. Big tits. Milky white skin. British. Artist. Used the sunroom as a studio. Lying naked on a flat lounge chair. Being fucked by a black guy with the biggest dick ever.

Rock was hard. He silently tiptoed across the room and dragged over his desk chair. Tasha's screams came hard and fast. He sat down. Undid his pants. And began to jerk off.

21

Rock lay there for a few minutes after he'd satisfied himself. Pulling off took quite the effort. This had been his third orgasm in eight hours. He went downstairs, opened a bottle of Merlot, and turned on a hockey game. The Kings were blowing a 3-1 lead against Anaheim. Less than ten minutes later, Tasha appeared, in her bra and panties. Without a word she poured herself a glass of wine and plunked herself down next to Rock.

"How's the painting going?" he said, without glancing away from the game.

"Terrible," she said, in her posh British accent. "I got nothing done today."

"Sorry," said Rock, "I didn't catch that. By whom did you say you were done today?"

Tasha leaned over and punched his arm. "You saw me, didn't you?"

"Yes. And the rest of the neighborhood heard you."

She blushed. "You're such a pervert."

"You could have closed the blinds."

"Sure." She leaned over and put her arms around him. This was not the first time she had watched a Kings game with Rock. Even though she knew absolutely nothing about hockey.

"Where's your husband?" he asked.

"In New Hampshire."

"What happened? He doesn't love you?"

"His father's dying. Dr. Motumbo came over to express his condolences. He was shocked to find out my father-in-law hadn't croaked yet. Then he asked if there was anything he could do, so I led him to the back porch."

"Uh-huh."

"I only had sex because I was curious. His wife and I had a discussion at a party once. About his anatomy."

"And it turned out to be true?"

"Yes. His cock was gigantic."

"You like that?"

"No, not at all. I could only get half of him in. I like to be pounded, you know, by a man's pelvic bone. All but impossible with the bone doctor. Unless I wanted to be impaled. Still, he was happy. I guess he doesn't get much attention from the white girls."

"Can I make a confession?"

She grabbed the remote for the monitor and muted it. "What?"

"I jerked off watching the two of you."

She grabbed his wine glass and put it on the coffee table. Then took his hands and rubbed them against her breast.

Rock sighed. "It's been a long day."

"You're no fun." She grabbed her glass of wine. "Have you heard the news?"

"No. I'm in a bubble for fifteen hours a day."

"Your country might be getting three new states. They've decided to have plebiscites. Canada is slowly taking over America. Like a virus. Or a glacier."

"I doubt that. They just want better health insurance. Besides, Quebec's having another referendum, too. Now that Washington State wants to join, the French-speaking minority will get even smaller. The last thing they want is more English speakers."

"Sounds like a total mess."

"Besides, none of these states will ever leave. It's all a tactic to express their dissatisfaction. They'll think twice when they see our gun laws."

"Maybe they should just kill the border. It'll make buying maple syrup so much easier."

"Yeah, but Canadians don't want the Mexicans coming up. They're worried we'll become like Texas. They only want rich immigrants. Like you. He took a sip of wine. Do you have any mandrakes?"

Tasha smiled. "On me?"

"Yeah."

She slipped her hand into her bra, producing a small packet with four pills. "I figured you might be out. I took your last one the other day. It's why I came over."

Rock clicked off the hockey once they washed down the tablets with a refill of wine. They cuddled together, all woozy. Rock felt great.

"Can I sleep here tonight?"

"Sure. As long as your husband doesn't barge in."

22

Vivian got to the studio early. The guard's clock said quarter after three in the morning. She couldn't imagine spending one more minute lying next to Doug. He'd gone out the previous night and gotten completely hammered. Knowing full well he'd have a miserable day today. Looking all puffy and horrible on camera. When he finally collapsed into bed around nine-thirty he had pawed at her. The last thing she had felt like doing was making love to a drunk.

Then, just after two, Finnegan had started barking. Vivian did, unlike many other dog owners, set limits on where he could run around. Her bedroom was off limits. She did not want to be in the physical act of love only to see Finnegan's puppy dog eyes staring up at her. Call her a prude.

She headed to makeup, and who did she find already there, with this month's Glamour in her hands, but Cindy Zhang. "What are you doing here?" asked Vivian.

"Renata called in sick. I'm doing the weather today."

"Really? What happened?"

"She had an allergic reaction to something. Broke out in hives. So I'm here for the next three days."

Vivian sat down in the adjacent makeup chair. Made small talk while she waited for the makeup woman to finish on Cindy. What a bitch, she thought during a lull in their conversation. Coming in early. She knew Cindy was gunning for her job on the traffic desk. Of course, it didn't help that they had the same last name. Vivian was convinced that Mel, their aging executive producer, had only hired Cindy because he thought she and Vivian were cousins. Or something.

Despite the fact that they were both of Chinese descent, Cindy had undergone substantial surgical alterations on her cheekbones and chin. To make herself look more like a white girl. To Vivian she looked fresh off the boat from Mexico. Ask any girl with Asian parents about the insecurity that arises around the topic of single-lidded eyes. Vivian didn't care, since she had double lids. At high school in Irvine she'd had blond-haired female friends and Asian female friends. All in the same social circle. Race wasn't something she paid attention to until much later in college. Until she'd learned of other Asians in her journalism class who had planned their eyelid surgery for the moment they turned eighteen. The whole thing was ridiculous.

Cindy also tanned. Like an obsessive white-girl. Her skin was dark enough naturally. Yet it was clear a recent trip to some spray-tan place had turned her into a fucking pumpkin. Vivian was careful not to point this out.

"But I don't understand," said Cindy, "the difference between the cabbage and the grapefruit diet."

"Huh?" said Vivian. She was still groggy, barely having taken more than a few sips of her coffee.

"They say that the grapefruit is supposed to speed up your metabolism. People on certain medications aren't supposed to eat it. But I'm thinking, maybe if I added it to my diet, I could lose some weight."

Vivian looked over at her. She was already rail-thin.

"But other people say the cabbage diet is better."

"As in…?"

"You just eat a lot of cabbage before meals. It fills you up so you eat less. And it has almost no calories."

"It also makes you fart."

"Everything has its downsides. By the way…"

She didn't stop, thought Vivian.

"Me and a bunch of the girls from the Palisades are going to Pasadena on Sunday afternoon."

"That's pretty far away for you guys."

"It is, but it has the best Hiroshima-yaki restaurant in the entire Southland. You should really come with us."

"That's tempting." Vivian loved Japanese food. But no way in hell would she spend more than five seconds with Cindy and her vapid circle of friends. She had done that last year. Once was enough. It didn't help

107

that Vivian was a few years older. Making her feel like the odd person out. Then there was the fact that Cindy constantly demanded she be the center of attention.

The makeup woman moved over to Vivian.

Cindy glanced over. "Oh, look at you, those marks around your eyes..."

"You mean the crows feet?" said Vivian. "Yes, they're always pressuring me to do my segment with a bag over my head."

23

Rock arrived on set half an hour late. Dougie had rolled up to his house at the correct time, but waited in vain. Eventually he knocked on the front door. Getting no answer, he walked inside, discovering Rock and Tasha naked on the couch. They had awoken earlier, made love, then fallen back asleep. It took much prodding by Dougie to get Rock to stir. Rock slipped him a week's worth of wages for his troubles—and his silence. And made a phone call explaining the situation to production.

Perhaps it was Rock's way of protesting against getting called in an extra day. There is only one thing that matters if you work on a film set. You must never, ever be late. One of the daily ADs tracked him down as he wandered to his trailer. Brought him to makeup. The crew seemed overly indifferent to him today.

Simpson was turning them against him. That had to be it.

The AD let him get a coffee, then escorted him to the prop table. Simon was the main guy. He'd been working on the production for months. "I left the bomb in your trailer."

Rock was still half-asleep. "You left what?"

"It's a mock up. There's a scientist to explain it all to you. But we're still waiting for him to show up. Everything's chaos today."

"Because I showed up late?"

"No, no one cares about that. We've got bigger problems. One of the execs showed up after they got a call from your agent. I heard screaming between Simpson and the producers. There's talk that he might be fired."

Rock rolled his eyes. "What good is that going to do now?"

"Exactly. You don't fire the director on the final day. Unless Disney's making the movie." Simon grabbed some prop guns out of his truck. Put them on his table.

"What's next after this?"

"For me?" said Simon. "Moving on to do a puppet show. Up in Toronto."

"That's a change."

"Actually, it's way more complicated. It's just me and another guy from up there. But it's inside. Air-conditioned. All on bluescreen. Way easier than worrying if my stuff'll show up on an international flight."

"You guys were sweating your balls off in Thailand."

"Oh, yeah. So, are you heading back to Canada?"

"Looks like it. I'm not much of an L.A. guy."

"I know. I have a newborn. My wife's not happy, but what are you going to do? I guess they have a nice hotel for all of us to stay at. Near the train station. Do you know where to get a decent steak in Toronto?"

"It's hit and miss, unless you pay through the nose. You're better off heading out to the suburbs. Good Indian and Chinese. If you like beef, you got to find a gig in Calgary. They know what they're doing out there."

"Really?"

"It's the Texas of the north. Just friendlier, with fewer churches. In the city, at least." Something caught Rock's eye by the studio door. Samantha. He needed to talk to her. He turned to Simon. "I gotta go. If I don't make it to the wrap, good luck with the puppets."

Rock followed Samantha to her seat in the video village. It was set up right near the camera. Simpson was away, setting up a scene with Shavon and the Louie guy from Hong Kong.

He sat down in the chair next to her. Simpson's chair. "Hey, can I talk to you?"

She looked over at him. Her face like slate.

"Just come outside for a sec."

"Whatever it is, you can say it in front of the crew. I'm busy. I can't leave the monitors. Can't this wait until lunch?"

"I might be gone by then."

She closed her laptop. "What do you want?"

"I wanted to say… I enjoyed working with you. And I like you. You're wonderful. I just don't think this can go any further."

"What exactly do you mean?" she screamed. "Tell me. Right to my face." The entire crew whipped their heads around. "You think you can use me like a fucking rag doll?"

"Please be quiet," said Rock, through clenched teeth.

"I'm just your sex toy? Fuck me every day in your trailer, then never see me outside of work? I have feelings too, you know. Let's be quite frank. You fucked me because your wife wasn't in town, and you were feeling horny."

"I never promised you anything. What the fuck is it with you…you… American women? Can't you have any fun without a lifetime commitment? We had an agreement."

"Everything's like a goddamn contract with you."

Rock sighed. He slinked out of the chair, and left. A defeated man.

24

"What you must understand completely," said Dr. von Stroheim, "is that the fuse housing connects to the firing mechanism. Okay?"

Rock and von Stroheim, the elderly scientist from the Jet Propulsion Lab in Pasadena, stood over the large plastic sphere that was on the floor in front of Rock's dining table.

"Isn't there just a lever to shut it off?"

"Yes, right here." von Stroheim pointed to a small black T-lever at the right of several dials. "But in the case of this weapon it has been modified to fail. So you have to undo the socket panel and access the wiring. By cutting the correct wire, the circuit is broken. Current will not reach the firing pin. The power will only engage the safety cutoff."

"Uh-huh."

1980 "The Year The Past Disappeared"

From the counter, von Stroheim grabbed a pair of pliers. "This is the most common device design for American technology. The reaction starts when this needle hits a peg. Connects to the firing mechanism. This is shielded by the radome, which houses the fusing, and the safety cutoff. Finally you have the firing unit. This is covered by ablative shielding, while inside of that is a layer of molded boron. Once the inverters are shut down by the altimeter, the electric current discharges, connects with the initiator conduct, these two elements come together inside the boron casing—"

"Sorry, doc, but I don't need a lesson in nuclear physics. I know you think you've got to earn your paycheck, but I just need to know what you want me to do."

"This model has been built to scale."

"But we're not showing it all on camera."

"I know, because of national security, and all that. But they were insistent that I explain all this to you, so please have patience and listen. In this scene, you will be disconnecting the bomb after it has been activated."

"Okay..." Rock looked over the sphere. "Look, I think I'm in over my head."

"Do not worry, it is very simple. They built the mechanism with safety in mind. Even a private in the army could diffuse one of these. In an emergency. Flying over the ocean in heavy turbulence. You understand? It can be done with a pair of pocket pliers. Hell, you could rip it out by hand, as long as you're careful."

"All this... is connected by a couple of wires?"

"Nuclear weapons are not that sophisticated. They are a 1940's technology, you know. There has been no need to make the firing mechanism more sophisticated. Why? It would require more people to work it. Which could lead to more leaks of technology. There's never been a need to add digital components. If we made it any more complicated, a foreign power could hack into it. Maybe make it do strange things. The actual rockets are controlled by smart-systems. But the bomb fuse hasn't changed in seventy years. The only addition is that many modern nuclear devices have remote count-down monitors that you can plug into a digital device. But it only keeps track of the timer. It can't prime or diffuse the detonator. You must either do that by hand. Or in a missile, it's done by gravity. Or by a lever activated by the rocket's computer, in cooperation with the gravitational system. So the warhead doesn't explode while stationary."

"So how do I turn it off?"

von Stroheim flipped up several panels. Until he reached a knot of multicolored wire. "This is very important. First, you rip out the purple wire." He tugged at it with some pliers. "Then the orange wire. In that order. If you do it the other way around, the bomb will not diffuse, understand? It's the same for every nuclear device made in the U.S.A." von Stroheim shut all the panels and handed the pliers to Rock. Now you try."

Rock looked at the bomb. He had completely forgotten everything von Stroheim had told him. The mandrakes had robbed him of his short-term memory.

25

It was impossible for anyone to ignore the bandage on Simpson's nose. Shavon leaned over to Rock. "I saw the makeup people putting it on this morning. Got here early and popped my head in the trailer. Saw them applying it."

"What?"

"He's wearing it for sympathy."

"Why?"

"He doesn't want to get fired."

The two of them were standing over the mock up of the nuclear bomb. Two assistants had lugged it from Rock's trailer to the set. Shavon's character was to help him diffuse it. "He wants to make your behavior the issue. Should the movie end up in the toilet."

"You've got to be joking."

"I'm serious. He actually believes this shit will be his get out of jail free card." Shavon pulled out her sides for a last minute check. "After a couple of months in the cutting room, no one will care about you. They'll be more worried why they spent so much on horses that they can't see through the smoke."

The makeup and wardrobe people did their final checks. The focus puller got out his measuring tape.

Rock felt impatient. "Why are we even doing this? It wasn't in the script."

"Simpson wants options for the final scene. The studio forced it on him because they didn't think the original ending had enough tension."

"We're going to be back in two months for re-shoots. I guarantee it."

"Okay, everyone," said Cochese, "picture's up." The crew went through their motions.

"Action!" yelled Simpson.

The scene began. This was when Rock realized he couldn't remember a single one of his lines. Every time Shavon spoke he responded with verbal diarrhea.

"Cut! What the hell, Rock?" yelled Simpson.

He had no idea. Rehearsal had gone perfectly. Perhaps too perfectly. They did the scene again. Rock resorted to asking for help from Samantha.

After five takes, Simpson walked over. "What do you want me to do? It's your job to learn your lines."

Rock glared at him. "Fine. We'll do it Italian-style. Like Fellini. I'll say one-two-three-four. Or I'll read the fucking phone book. You can overdub it in post. Keep to the wide."

"I need a close up."

"Too bad. Those lines are filled with technobabble. You've pissed me off so much in the last three days that I don't give a rat's ass. Do the scene with my stand in, if you want."

"Your job—"

"Shut up or I walk."

26

Rock was exhausted as he sauntered over to his trailer. Still, he refused a ride from transport. Walking was pretty much his only form of exercise. They had done four scenes in a row with the nuclear bomb mock up. With no changes in the set up. Although they did have a camera on a dolly.

Shavon had her lines down pat. Rock had mouthed numbers he remembered for pizza delivery. The soundman had taken them aside after the scene and recorded a clean track away from the cameras. Just as a backup. Simpson had sunk into a deep depression, which amused Shavon to no end.

The producers didn't share her sense of humor. But they were impressed that Simpson got through six pages in a single morning. Even with two cameras, that was a remarkable amount of material. Rock hadn't shot that much since the days when he used to guest star on series television. But in the back of his head he knew it would probably have to be re-shot. The editor would find some problem with it.

Usually, at the end of a long shoot, Rock would be greeted with hugs and handshakes from the crew. A general feeling of sadness that the production was coming to an end. Not today. Rock was done, but everyone else had a couple more days. For pickups. It was still an open question of whether Rock was going to attend the wrap party. His animosity towards Simpson might outweigh his clamoring for free booze.

He passed the makeup trailer. People were busy. No one seemed to notice him. Rock wanted to get out of here as fast as possible, so he left the makeup people in peace.

When he got to his trailer, Ira was waiting for him. "Hey," said Rock, "what's going on?"

"Are you out of your fucking mind?"

"Huh?"

"It's already on the Enquirer's website. The whole recording."

"What are you talking about?"

"That little display of affection with the continuity girl this morning? Someone recorded it."

"Who would have..."

"What's her name? Samantha? You are aware that her laptop gets a feed from the video assist and the comdexes, right? Maybe she leaked it. Or that dickhead director. You DID physically assault him."

Rock sat down, devastated. "This is not happening."

"You're supposed to keep these things quiet—"

"I did. Do you think I'm some kind of asshole?"

"We have to be very honest about this. Your career is sliding downhill. When I take the job as president of this studio, I'll be on your side. But there are a lot of people who won't. They don't want to see you in movies anymore. That's the real reason why you have nothing lined up. We made a lot of money the last ten years. But your face was on too many things. Is that my fault? Probably."

"I was hoping you'd still be gunning for me."

"Of course. But when you pull shit like this, I can't protect you against the other members of the board."

"I need a drink."

"No. Don't start drinking. We don't need you crashing Christmas trees, like you did in Melbourne last year. Go home. Smoke a joint. Get under the covers. Then tomorrow, call your wife. Take the hit. Tell her everything. Give her some time, if need be."

"What if she wants a divorce? I have children."

"Time is your friend. The movie won't come out until next year."

"I'm supposed to fly out to Cape Breton tomorrow night. What will she say if I stay here?"

"She's angry. And humiliated. Remember that you are the guilty party, not her."

"That's your best advice?"

"No, there's one thing you can say that might help."

"What?"

1980 "The Year The Past Disappeared"

"Tell your wife you were paying the continuity girl for her services. When she demanded a bonus at the last minute, you wouldn't pay up. Say she threatened you with the tape. But you stood your ground, rather than give in to an extortionist."

"That's the most ridiculous plan I've ever heard."

"Hey, it saved my marriage."

27

One of the dirty little secrets of Rock's career is that he'd never actually seen anything he'd been in. Even if he was obligated to attend a premier, he would tactfully exit the theater the moment the movie began. On occasions with a post-screening Q & A, that meant two hours in a bar while the picture screened.

He was very self-conscious about hearing his voice. And his double chin. Not to mention his graying sideburns. Now, listening to his conversation with Samantha, he felt sick. Hearing the disdain and the pleading in his voice. It cut through him like a knife.

Something deep inside of him didn't believe this was happening. Even so, his practical side kicked in. He called Larry, his accountant in Vancouver.

"Listen," said the man who had filed his taxes for the past five years, "your assets are relatively simple. You've got the house, and that's about it. Most people with money have their hands in a lot more cookie jars."

"What about the Yugoslavian stuff?"

"That's sheltered in a bank. If it hasn't come onto your wife's radar, you're only dealing with the cash in your bank accounts here. Plus your index funds and bonds. And your pension fund. But she has to keep in mind that those investments will take a tax hit when they're sold. You don't have any losses for the last five years." Rock heard Larry shuffling through papers. "One more thing, do you have any history of clinical depression? Any record of counseling?"

"No. Why?"

"When I got divorced, that allowed me to get a much more generous financial agreement. Just saying."

"I don't think that'll work for me." They made some more small talk, before Rock ended the conversation.

Then he bit the bullet and phoned his wife. Candy was already on the computer. She answered on the first ring. It was already almost half past five in the Maritimes.

"Thank you for answering." Rock looked at her eyes. She'd been crying.

She spoke in Mandarin. "I knew there was always a ring of truth to the rumors. Do you want a divorce?"

"I don't think this is the time to discuss this."

"Oh, really? Then when will be? My parents will hear about this. You've humiliated me."

"Please, you don't expect your father to care—"

"And the rest of my family?"

"There's nothing I can do about it."

"How many times did you go to bed with her?"

"Once."

"You're lying. Is she the only one?"

"Yes. What can I say? I was lonely. We had an agreement. If we were in different cities."

"And we agreed not to tell each other. If I cheated on you, I wouldn't publish it in the newspaper."

"Look," said Rock, "you get all the benefits of a comfortable life with lots of money. Okay? Even if you divorce me. You're set for the rest of your life. But part of being married to a public figure is that you're going to have to deal with the humiliating rumors and press. Those people are dogs."

"I don't care."

"What do you want me to do? Do you want me to come back?"

"I have to pick the children up from piano lessons in ten minutes. We'll talk later."

And with that, she ended the connection.

28

"I hate you."

"What do you mean?" said Doug. "Why are you getting so angry about this?"

Vivian and Doug had barricaded themselves in the makeup room.

"Look," he said, "let's be honest, you've aged since the wedding."

"It's all because of you. The stress of having to support you, bumbling through interviews."

"Please, don't be so—"

"And you always have this pleading way about you. Like you don't deserve me."

"Look, I'm sorry—"

"Stop saying you're sorry. Why do you have to always be such a...a... beta...male?"

Doug clenched his teeth. "This is not about me,

this is about you. Your sense of self-worth. Just because I mix up one Z-list Hong Kong actor from another doesn't make me a racist." He sat down in the makeup chair next to her and took her hands in his. "I married you because I love you. But whatever you need to feel better about, you've got to find it within yourself." He leaned back. "There are some things you can do. They have many clinics around town. You'd be surprised how good women can look, even when they're over forty."

"I'm thirty-three." Vivian recoiled from him. "This is unbelievable." She stood up, and ran out, leaving Doug and Finnegan behind. She burst through the door, saw the crowd of people waiting for their argument to finish.

"Fuck off, all of you."

Doug followed her. "Don't treat people like this."

Vivian stormed out to the parking lot and got into her car. Doug was still on her. "You've got to calm down. I'm the one going through a tough time right now. Not you."

"Oh, stop, will you? You're such an embarrassment." She turned her back to him and got in the car. Peeled out of the parking lot as Doug watched helplessly.

She headed down to the 101. Got stuck in a traffic jam headed to North Hollywood. Why was she driving towards the valley? She turned off the highway in Studio City. At least no one will be looking for me here, Vivian thought. She pulled into the back of a Ralphs parking lot.

She felt frazzled. Like she wanted to get away from everything. She hit the tint button on the dash. Doug had paid extra for it because the feature changed the color of the glass to an opaque white, keeping the interior of the parked car cool on hot days. It also allowed privacy in case of intimate in-car moments, which she suspected was his real reason for spending the extra money.

Then Vivian shut off the engine. Leaned her forehead against the steering wheel. And broke down in tears. She was thirty-four years old. Part of her wanted to have a child. But the other part wanted to anchor the evening news. That had been her dream since she was a child. Watching Connie Chung on CBS. Her earliest career role model.

Vivian was beginning to think the whole morning traffic job was a dead end. She'd been getting up at three a.m. for six years. It was killing her. The wrinkles were just one sign of it. Was this really something she wanted to do for the next twenty years?

Then there was her husband. She loved Doug. But they'd both be a lot happier if she didn't have to see him every day at work. To be married and on the job together takes a certain personality, something she wasn't sure she possessed.

Her phone buzzed. Doug had sent her an appointment for a skin care clinic. An appointment for that afternoon. And a note: "Los Angeles is the only market in the world where the 4 a.m. news is widely watched. All those people working on film sets need to know about freeway accidents. You're like the Elvis of early-morning traffic reporters. I'll take you out to dinner tonight."

1980 "The Year The Past Disappeared"

Vivian couldn't help but smile at Doug's message. He was so clueless it was endearing. Another woman might have felt insulted, but Vivian knew he meant well. She clicked on the link. The clinic was near Hollywood Center station. In this traffic it would take her an hour to get there.

Vivian started the car. The electric engine hummed strangely. Then came a grinding sound. The whole thing shut off. She opened her door. Steam was billowing out of the hood.

This was becoming a very, very bad day. She picked up her phone and searched for a tow truck.

29

Rock made an appointment with the stem cell clinic. Part of him wondered if he could get plastic surgery to hide his identity. He'd disappear. Become a novelist. Or a mime.

He dressed out of his costume and filled in some paperwork. Took one last check around the trailer he'd inhabited for the past few weeks. The scene of the crime, as it were. Dougie was waiting out front, in the same car with the broken dampening field. They exchanged greetings, and departed the parking lot where the unit was set up. They drove around the studio, down one of the back roads.

"Hey," said Rock, "listen, you can just drop me off at the bottom of the street."

"I don't know, sir, the producer gave me special orders that I was to drive you all the way home, no matter what."

This was typical. Part of the production's insurance on him. Rock dug into his wallet and took out one of his business cards. "Here, take this. Shoot me a message when you're done your script. But only once you're sure it's as perfect as it can be. Send it to other people you trust and get their opinions. Then make sure you fix all the spelling errors. When that's done, send it to me. I might want to direct it."

"You? A director?"

"Well, my acting career's not exactly on the upswing. This is something you don't know yet, but you're going to learn. You and I are almost in the same boat. Don't kid yourself. We're all working dad-to-day in this business." Rock flipped through his wallet and took out a wad of bills. Passed it to Dougie. "Drop me off at the bottom of the hill. Take the money. Keep quiet and relax for a couple of hours. Just make it look like you dropped me off in Santa Monica, okay?"

"Gee, thanks, Mr. MacLean."

"Don't drop me off on the main road, turn down one of these side streets."

Dougie picked a residential street heading towards the hills. A mixture of bungalows and gated driveways that led up to upper-middle-class dwellings. With lavish foliage.

Rock said goodbye and got out. For the first time in several months, he felt free. No obligations. No one to go home to. And nobody cared.

He wandered up the street. Gazing at the homes. Normal life in north Los Angeles. He was the only one around except for some landscapers.

The sound of a buzz saw growled out from behind a nearby house. It triggered a memory of a few weeks previous. In his neighborhood which straddled the border between Venice and Santa Monica. An angry man with no shirt had been wandering the beach with a chain saw. Fortunately the police had gotten to him before he could do any harm. Not much comfort for the dozens of people he'd scared the shit out of. That, in a nutshell, was what L.A. was kind of like. At least to Rock. Enough crazy people to keep you slightly on edge. The heat and the terrible state of the American mental health system had a lot to do with it, no doubt.

There was a time when Rock wanted to be a director, like Werner Herzog. Or Samuel Fuller. Make amazing films, chronicling your era. And the people living in it. Interspersed with documentaries about fascinating subjects. Something that film critics would look at and call important.

But his career had descended very abruptly to the point where in every film he played either a general, a soldier or a spy. Which were fun roles. But he longed to do something artistic. Something where he had to act, as opposed to just showing up. But that could lead to embarrassment, which is why Ira had always counseled against it. With The Man in the High Castle, even though he was in nearly every scene, the role was something he could pull off blindfolded and tied to a chair. He'd played it ten times before.

Rock's cell phone buzzed. It was Pantha. His drug dealer.

"Hey, you."

135

"Hello. Good to get a hold of you so easily." The young man spoke with a thick Swiss-German accent. "It seems your water is in."

"What?" Rock stopped in his tracks. Miracle of miracles. "You've just made my day."

"It was a once-in-a-decade opportunity. I couldn't let it fall through my fingers. Must be all those Chinese bomb factories. It seems a shipment has crossed the ocean and landed here."

"How much is it going to cost me?"

Pantha rattled off a number that would buy you a nice low-end luxury vehicle. "And please bring it in cash," he added.

"No problem." Rock could stop at the bank. He loved carrying wads of money. He would take the subway. Criminals didn't expect the wealthy people of Southern California to ride public transit.

After a few more words, he ended the call and bounded down the street. Ecstatic. He had to find a bank.

Then his phone rang again.

"Hi there," came a woman's pleasant voice, "my name's Loreen, calling from Dr. Park's office. We've managed to squeeze you in, if you can make it here by two o'clock."

Rock checked his watch. He had forty-five minutes. He might just make it. But he really wanted to see Pantha first. "Is there any way I could schedule an appointment for tomorrow?"

"I'm afraid not. We had two cancellations because of a late flight. The next opening isn't for three weeks."

This doctor was good. Rock had no choice. He might be back in Cape Breton by then. "Fine. I'll see you at two."

He headed towards the subway.

Then another call. Rock stopped. He didn't like to walk and talk. It was Ira.

"I thought you disowned me."

Ira laughed. "You wish. Look, me and Danielle are having a barbecue tomorrow. I expected you to be gone out of town by now, so I didn't mention it. Drop by. I'll send you the invite. It's my going away party from the agency. And my welcoming party to the studio."

"You said you wanted me to hide."

"I do. But I also want you to see my new house. It's where Orson Welles died. With a typewriter on his stomach. And you get to show people you're a human being, not just a headline. It takes balls to go out in public with what you're going through."

"Or stupidity."

30

Rock broke into a jog. He wanted to get to the station. But also, he wanted to check out what looked like a pretty good-looking girl in a tight blue dress that had just headed down the steps a hundred meters ahead of him. Even in the depths of despair, he still had a roving eye.

He headed to the southbound platform of the Vermont line. The train was just pulling in. He managed to catch up with the girl in the blue dress. The train wasn't crowded. He got a seat right across from her.

As per usual, she gave him a long gaze. It was the exact length of time it took the person to decide whether Rock was a celebrity or not. He had yet to get used to it. If it was a man, or an ugly girl, he did his best to ignore them. Earlier in his career there were times when such stares really ticked him off. But after three or four years of being famous he'd mellowed, and resigned himself to this fate.

The flipside was he got lots of attention from pretty girls. He always had. Still, some refused to look at him at all. Maybe they didn't want to seem too obvious. This girl, however, looked familiar. He couldn't quite place her. She was certainly stylishly dressed. Maybe she'd worked on a show with him?

The train's speakers crackled. "The next station is Hollywood Central. Please change here for the Hollywood Line, the Santa Monica Line, the La Brea line, the Ventura regional commuter line, the Inglewood Airport Rapid Express, the Amtrack bullet train and the Rapid Service Sunset Boulevard-Beverly Center Monorail Line. The doors on the right side will open." The message repeated in Spanish.

Rock and blue dress girl locked eyes. After a couple of moments he got distracted by his phone. Quarter to two. Rock stood up and headed to the doors. In the dark reflection off the window he snuck another look. He hoped she wasn't an insane person.

The train rumbled into the station. The doors opened. Rock beckoned to the woman in blue. "Ladies first."

She smiled and passed him by. "Thank you."

Very cute, he thought. And in a short hemline. Even if he got divorced, maybe there was hope. Then he shook his head and walked onto the platform. He let the woman get well ahead of him.

Behave yourself, Rock.

31

Vivian couldn't believe it. She'd gotten the attention of Rock MacLean. In a town of actors, he was the face at the top of the totem pole right now. And he was actually good-looking, too. Surprising for a man his age. Often male celebrities were admired by the camera, but in real-life they often turned out to be short. Or have a freakishly big head. If it actually was Rock MacLean. It might be his doppelganger. From Omaha or someplace. Still, he looked like everything Doug wasn't.

She reached the stairs to the northeast exit. Vivian looked back and saw the man was following her. Discreetly, but still behind her.

It couldn't be him, the voice sounded wrong. Why would he be taking public transit?

She emerged onto Hollywood Boulevard. Throngs of tourists crowded the street. Checking her phone, she noticed she was early. Public transport in Los Angeles. It was almost too punctual, wasn't it? She stopped at a flower shop, to cool off for a moment. The sun had come out, and was beating down on the sidewalk.

When she emerged, she saw the same man was loitering around the deli next door.

That was weird. She turned the corner. Another block to go. The clinic was in a building on the other side of Franklin. She looked back. The guy who looked like Rock MacLean turned a corner. It was only her and him on the side street.

This made her nervous.

She walked into the courtyard of an old 1920's-era apartment building. The clinic was on the first floor. As she opened the door, she saw the MacLean wannabe wander into the complex. There was no question he was coming after her.

The waiting room was deserted. Vivian ran up to the receptionist. "Call the police. I'm being pursued by a stalker."

32

Loreen, the receptionist, looked up at Vivian. "Excuse me?"

"There's a man following me. Call the police."

The chime on the door sounded. Loreen looked over. "Ah, Mr. MacLean. The doctor is ready to see you. Have a seat." She turned to Vivian. "You too, ma'am."

Vivian sat down next to Rock. "Sorry, I saw you following me and got nervous."

Rock smiled. "No problem. There's all kinds of crazy people out there."

Vivian giggled nervously.

Loreen approached with clipboards and forms for them to fill out. Vivian welcomed the distraction. "Sorry," she said, laying her hand on his arm, "are you really Rock MacLean? The actor?"

"The same, dear lady."

"Is this place the secret to looking young?"

"That, and they put power windows on my wrinkles in post. I have it written into my contract."

"I see."

He gazed at her face. "You know, you look awfully familiar."

"I'm on a morning show—"

"You do the traffic updates on KXXX."

"Exactly."

"I owe you big time. You don't know how many times you've saved my neck. I'm so sleepy when I leave my house, if I'm shooting. And you have that cute dog..."

"Yeah, Finnegan."

"He's an Akita, right?"

"Yeah. From Japan."

"I used to live there."

"Wow."

"Yeah."

"So, this place is good to get rid of wrinkles?"

"Actually, it's for my hair. If it weren't for Dr. Park, I'd look a lot like Patrick Stewart."

Vivian giggled. "No, you're way cuter."

Rock rolled his eyes. "Stop. You're mocking me— "

"No, I mean it."

"So why are you here? You don't look like you need any help looking beautiful."

"The station is getting these new 10K cameras next month. They make every wrinkle look like the Grand Canyon."

"They must have diffusion to put over the lens."

"I wish. But we're live. They won't do it. It's all those early mornings."

"Hey... didn't your husband do that interview—"

"With your co-star? Yeah. Doug is a bit of a nitwit sometimes. That's why they put him on at five a.m."

"Mr. MacLean?" said Loreen. "The doctor will see you."

Rock stood up. "Nice to meet you." He shook her hand. "And don't tell anyone I was here."

She smiled. "Our secret."

Rock was greeted in the examination room by Dr. Park, one of the leading cosmetic cellologists in the world. The elderly Korean man gestured for him to sit down on a lowered stool.

"Very good," he said, examining Rock's scalp. "It seems the cells have taken hold. Any problems with itching or dandruff?"

"Nothing."

"Excellent. I don't think you'll need to see me for another six months. How are things going?"

"Good."

"I see."

"Actually not so good."

"I heard. That's why I cleared my schedule."

"Really?"

"I had to make sure the treatment wasn't making you suicidal."

"Why would it do that?"

"Stem cells are not fully understood. They have strange properties. At least when applied to acne. On teenagers."

"What?"

Park nodded. "Nothing you need to worry about."

"How are your kids?"

"Good. Steven's about to start at Occidental College this September. He's all excited."

"Staying at home?"

"It's close by. How old are your girls now?"

"The oldest is starting school in September."

"That's great."

A silence hung in the room for far too long. "I don't know what I'm going to do," said Rock. "Maybe this is all my fault. Like I'm doing things on purpose. To cause a divorce."

"Well, we're all a little guilty, aren't we?"

"I'm worried I might be out of control."

"That's a normal feeling."

"It is?"

"You're a tall, powerful man who is a wealthy celebrity. But the money's the kicker. I used to go to three whores a week when my wife was nursing our children. She didn't ask any questions. And I didn't volunteer any answers."

"But she feels betrayed—"

"If you can let go of the guilt, your marriage will survive. But if you keep thinking you've betrayed her, and that's all you see when you look at her... well, even if she forgives you, you won't be able to accept that forgiveness. And it will ruin your sex life."

"So I should just put this out of my head? And soldier on?"

"Why not? But there are two main dangers with sleeping around when married. One, you might accidentally give your wife an STI."

"And?"

"You might fall in love with your mistress."

33

The Nicaraguans had hunkered down. For the last twenty-four hours they had occupied a basement apartment at the northern edge of Van Nuys. Spying on fifteen different drug dealers. All of whom they suspected of working with the Nigerians. Many of these dealers had sophisticated security set-ups. With cameras and motion detectors. Which made the Nicaraguan's job easier. One of the four men who had survived the attack was an expert at hacking security cameras.

One of the Nigerians had been arrested for impersonating an officer. That made tracking down their associates incredibly easy. Now the worry was that their surveillance had started too late.

Bushy eyebrows ate dinner with two of his men while another manned a computer, looking for movement.

The man at the computer yelled to them, excited.

Bushy eyebrows walked over. The screen was set up to display all fifteen cameras at once. The man pointed up to one of the corners. With a click he enlarged the video feed.

"Is that who I think it is?" said bushy eyebrows.

"Yes," said the man, "he's the actor."

"A kidnapping would really send a message. We could ransom him. Demand our product back."

They watched as Rock sat down on a couch at a fairly upscale house in West Hollywood.

"Shut that off. We go now."

The four men emerged from the basement, into the garage of the small suburban bungalow. They loaded their weapons into the Mercedes, which now had its bullet holes repaired and repainted.

Bushy eyebrows took the passenger seat. His associate turned on the car. Less than a second later there was a small explosion in the engine block. Steam wafted up in front of the windshield.

The driver got out and looked under the hood. "There's our problem. Broken radiator."

Bushy eyebrows looked over the engine. "Can you fix it?"

"Yes. But it will take time. I've got to get parts. We're not going anywhere tonight."

34

Rock had been to Pantha's house plenty of times before. He was a Swiss video artist who did a pretty good sideline as a drug dealer.

Pantha cleared the couch of oil paintings and cutouts from magazines. Rock found a space between old copies of Omni. "You really like the print stuff, don't you?"

"Digital bores me. If you can't hold it in your hands, what's the point? That's the reason I'm a drug dealer. I don't want to do websites. And other stupid graphic design. Like video games. The law may see me as a criminal, but I see myself as a person just trying to get by."

Pantha passed a joint over.

"Sure," said Rock, taking a puff. After exhaling, Rock pointed to him. "What's that?"

Pantha reached down and stretched out his white

T-shirt. In the center was a huge rectangle displaying a GIF. The shirt had display fibers woven into the cotton to show an animation. The Statue of Liberty's torch transformed into a golf club and began whacking away buildings from the Manhattan skyline.

"I got it from a cart vendor at Hollywood and Vine. You know how they're building a golf course in Central Park?"

"People are really upset about that. They're tearing down the Empire State Building."

"For real?"

"I've seen the plan. Unless they're going to build it underground."

"Thing is," said Pantha, taking the joint, "right after I bought this I saw a homeless guy, outside the Chinese theater. Begging for change from the tourists. He had one of these shirts. Playing a loop of a girl taking a shit. All the fat Midwesterners would walk up with their coins, take one look, and run off."

"That's disgusting. How was he even able to charge it? Homeless people don't pay for electricity."

"Must have a charger at the shelter. The police picked him up eventually."

"It's like those guys they arrested. On the beach in Venice last year. Hitting on chicks with porn playing on their shirts. Total fucking goons. What is it about this city that makes people go retarded?"

"I heard one of them actually got laid."

Rock laughed so hard he snorted.

"So," said Pantha, "I have something for you. He

handed over a half-liter bottle of clear liquid. You've got the money?"

"As requested." Rock took an envelope out of his pocket stuffed with cash. Handed it over.

While Pantha checked the bills, Rock launched an app on his phone. The camera flash shone a blue light through the plastic water bottle. Rock examined the results. Exactly within limits. He unscrewed the cap and drank it down. It tasted a bit strange. Almost like flavor-less milk. That was the best way he could describe it.

Pantha put the envelope away. "That should keep you going for a number of years. Cleans the liver cells right out."

"Who knew it would become so expensive."

"Blame fusion. They're shutting down all the small nuclear plants. And there isn't much of a market for it. People would rather eat their vegetables."

"I suppose."

Pantha stood up. "Can I show you something? I want your opinion."

Rock took another puff off the joint before handing over the roach. "I don't know. It's been a rough day. I might not be your ideal audience."

"So I've heard. Maybe this might cheer you up."

Pantha led him through a set of French doors. An area that must have been the house's dining room in a former life, but was now occupied by a large billiard table. He handed Rock a long extendable metal rod. At the end was a leather hand grip. Clearly Pantha had constructed it himself.

As Rock extended his rod, he realized what it was. "This is from—"

"An old style radio antenna. Pretty ingenious, eh?"

Pantha flipped a switch. There was a hum of a generator. The surface of the billiard table came alive. Rising up from it a holographic representation of East Asia. From a basket Pantha grabbed several small rubber balls, the size of marbles. He handed some to Rock.

"What is all this?"

"It's like billiards combined with Risk."

"You mean, the board game?"

"Yeah."

"I haven't played that in twenty years."

"Exactly. You be the Democrats, I'll be the Maoists. Each one of those rubber balls is an army battalion. See how the table is littered with small holes? Watch this."

Pantha placed one ball on Tianjian. Then moved around the table and placed another on Inner Mongolia. Using the radio antenna cue, he fired this ball at Tianjian. The hologram above the surface exploded with light and color. As the two balls collided, the space above them erupted with cartoon armies firing cartoon mortars at each other. The Tianjian ball dropped into a hole. An animated victory celebration commenced.

"That's quite impressive. But won't it get annoying?"

"It only does that the first couple of rounds."

"What are these towers set up by the Hong Kong and Shanghai Free States?"

"They're the X-factor positions. If you have extra players, like, say, your wife, they can man those towers. Randomly send out balls onto the table. To thwart both sides."

"What? In case your girlfriend gets bored? She can lose the game for you?"

"Exactly. Just like in a real war."

Rock smiled. "It's nice. As long as it doesn't turn out like those driverless cars you weaponized."

Pantha laughed. He never responded to the rumor that he had modified several of Google's self-driving cars. The kinds used for pizza delivery. He had added automatic weapons in place of the passenger side airbags. Turned them into death delivery machines. Soon after, the state of California had banned driverless cars. Now Google was trying to convince the government the concept would be safe on a modified highway. But no one really cared, not after all the money spent on bullet trains and subways.

"That was only a rumor," said Pantha. "Why would I do something like that?"

"Same reason I get in trouble with girls. You like the thrill of danger."

"I will say, I missed those driverless cars, especially the trucks."

"Why?"

"With the opacity on the windows up, they were great for screwing on the way to work."

This made Rock laugh.

35

Rock sat on his living room sofa, reading The Brothers Karamazov. He felt more refreshed than he had in years. Against the shadows in the corner of the room he saw the lights go on next door. Tasha was home.

He grabbed his phone and called her. "Why don't you come over?"

"Sure." She arrived a minute later, a white plastic bag in her hand. "I brought some extra sushi, if you want some."

Rock looked up from his tablet. For all of Tasha's artistic talent, her sense of aesthetics hit a wall when it came to food. "Take out? It won't kill me, will it?"

"I don't know. It's from the new place on Abbot Kinney."

After finishing off the mediocre balls of rice, smoked salmon, and cucumber wrapped in nori, Rock eyed her skimpy flower print dress.

She put down her chopsticks. Gazed into his eyes.

Rock stood up and took her hand. Led her to his bedroom.

They lay down on the bed and kissed for a few minutes. "You know," said Rock, pausing the action, "it seemed a lot easier to get laid once I got married."

"That's sort of the point."

"I meant with other women."

Tasha petted his nose. "Do you still love your wife?"

"I don't know." He caressed her body. Took off her dress. They made love effortlessly. Once they were done satisfying each other, they cuddled in the orange glow of the streetlight.

"Do you want to stay here tonight?" he asked.

"I can't," she said. "I'm worried he might come home."

"What happened?"

"His father got better. It doesn't look like we're getting the townhouse in Manhattan any time soon."

"All you want is real estate?" Rock was disappointed by her coldness towards her in-laws.

"Sure. All the land is opening up there. Those skyscrapers don't last forever."

Rock caressed her hair. "Everyone seems to have advice for me. I'm glad you accept me as I am."

"I don't know, love, your wife has been humiliated by your infidelity. She'll never get over that. Even if you don't get divorced."

"I wish there was something I could do."

"It's not a problem you can solve. Give her space. Let her figure it out on her own." She nuzzled his shoulder. "Why is it men always want to solve people's problems?"

"It's the engineer in each of us, I suppose."

Tasha climbed out of the bed and wandered to the stereo. She looked over Rock's playlists. Put on Under the Pink by Tori Amos. "I had no idea you were into her."

"I'm a closet Tori fan."

"Most heterosexual men are. Closeted, I mean."

"That's not amusing."

She sat down on the bed and wiggled his toes, like he was a child. "Just remember, time heals all wounds."

Rock lay back in his pillow and shut his eyes.

"And don't forget, love is a zero-sum game."

When he awoke two hours later she was gone.

36

Dewey sat at the console in his video room. He considered the machine his own work of art. Five monitors. Two keyboards. But the lynchpin was the control panel in the dead center of the desk. With arrays of buttons, dials, and switches.

An alert sounded. He looked up at the readout displayed on one of the monitors. All different colors. With a trackpad he brought up a graphic of the earth. Various orbits of satellites. He picked one and clicked on it. A progress bar appeared. Uploading commenced.

Finally, after five years of preparation. His plans were complete. In less than two minutes the satellite would be under his control.

Of course, he still had to be patient. He ran a few more calculations. Then set the timer. A countdown began. Seventy-one hours to go. Until his plan was complete. Twenty-four hours until stage one. The satellite would pass over Los Angeles tomorrow afternoon. At quarter after six. Right on time for the evening rush hour.

Friday evening. People would be exhausted from the workweek. They would be totally unprepared for what awaited them. The satellite's pulse coils would be hijacked by his programming. Leading to chaos.

He wandered to the bar in the next room and poured himself a nice tall glass of scotch. Everything was complete. He switched on the bar's remote monitor and watched the progress of the drill bit. It had performed better than Dewey's wildest hopes. Still going, at over seven hundred degrees Fahrenheit.

He took another sip of scotch and thought about what he was unleashing. Many times he had wondered if he had gone insane. But, after a couple of drinks and a good night's sleep, he decided that, yes, what he was doing was bad, but no, it wasn't immoral.

The human race had gone too far in the wrong direction. Maybe he, Dewey, was a natural catalyst. Like a forest fire clearing an excess of pine trees. Or a volcano erupting in the middle of a coral reef.

It was the same as the wars in Asia. Those governments had played god, creating a surplus of angry young men. Now their nations were battle scarred and burnt. The result of their eugenics programs, tacitly, if not officially, sponsored by the states themselves.

Dewey would rid more of Southern California's old and infirm, leaving resources to the young and strong.

Some people would survive. The city would be rebuilt. But that wasn't the point. Once Los Angeles was taken care of, Dewey was sure others would follow his lead. Realizing this was the only way out for their species.

It was the fact that he was a victim that gave him the fortitude to ignore conventional morality. He was well aware that many bleeding hearts would describe him as a murderer. But he felt justified.

Sometimes bad things had to happen.

37

Rock got up early the next day. He wandered around Santa Monica and avoided eating lunch. Ira's barbecue was smack dab in the center of Friday afternoon. Just in time to be used as an excuse to get off work early. At two o'clock he boarded the Santa Monica Line. Got off at the West Hollywood stop. Walked the final few blocks to the house.

He was greeted in the driveway by Ira's wife, Shelly.

"So good to see you, Rock," she said, in a not-all-that-convincing tone.

"Yeah. This is your new place?"

"We moved in two weeks ago." She led him around to the back yard. The party was in full swing.

"Quite the property you have here. Guesthouse and garage, I see. But it feels a lot smaller."

"The last of the kids are gone, so we figured we'd downsize. They still have rooms, if they need to sleep over. But less square footage to clean. Hopefully I won't miss the Palisades when the summer heat waves arrive. Of course, our children need their independence."

Rock peered over the crowds. A giant boxing ring had been set up in the corner of the yard. "What is that?"

"Oh... it's Ira's thing. Something the guys are into."

"Uh-huh."

"Why don't you help yourself to some food? We flew in Ira's favorite Greek chef."

Rock took his cue and wandered off through the crowds. Several faces looked familiar. Of course people were already staring at him. He tried to avoid their gazes with out pissing anyone off. Or getting pissed off himself. That was the art of celebrity.

He got in line for the buffet. Ahead of him were two junior executives at the studio. A fancy title for a fairly low-paying job. He made small talk about the dangers of automated cars with them. They seemed a bit star-struck by his presence.

The vast majority of the people looked like they were from Ira's agency. Still, he recognized a few faces from the High Castle crew. At the end of the line for food, he bumped into Lazlo, the director of photography.

"These new cameras," he said, "they are nothing but garbage."

"What do you mean?"

"They changed the codec. Again. So you can't get a proper black."

"There's no way to adjust it with the waveform monitor? Or in post?"

"It is more complicated than that." His thick Hungarian accent gripped the technical vocabulary. "Even at this late a date, image capture is mostly an analog process. When light enters the camera, it hits a sensor that is no different that those of fifty years ago. The digital components just sample the image. So the file size is smaller. But how it does the conversion makes all the difference. They've been increasing the resolution steadily, without caring about latitude and color fidelity. Engineers looking at nothing but numbers on a spreadsheet. Now they're going backwards. They ruin everything. Fixing what isn't broken."

Lazlo was like a walking library on cameras and lights. Rock enjoyed listening to his anecdotes and complaints.

Ira appeared, making his way through the crowds. "Well, look who it is. The scandal of the week."

Lazlo nodded and took off. He didn't like Ira, who had a reputation for abrasiveness.

Rock smiled. "This is an excellent roast lamb you're serving. The olives are nice, too."

"Yes, this guy came in all the way from Greektown in Toronto. I figured it would bring back memories."

"Well, you'd need some donair sauce, I suppose..."

Ira tapped on his phone. "I'm going to send you something right now. Read it soon. The file will self-destruct in three days. And you can't copy it, either. But it will really knock your socks off. You remember that director I told you about?"

"Campbell?"

"Yeah."

"You're out of your fucking mind."

"It's his secret diary."

"No."

"You said you wanted to do a cartoon. This is you, sitting in a booth, making enough money to buy a house. It'll take a week to record, tops. It's about the Fukushima earthquake in Japan."

"Charming."

"It's his secret diaries. But done as an animated film." Ira leaned in, lowering his voice to a whisper. "There's lots of sex in it. Some of it is pretty hot stuff." His eye caught someone behind rock. "Excuse me for a moment."

Rock ate his goat and feta salad. Lazlo sauntered over again. "You know his wife is drawing two salaries. One from the agency, and another from the studio. She's one of the producers on the Campbell project."

"Oh well. As long as I'm not going hungry, it doesn't bother me."

"Pays for a nice house. How come I never see your wife at these things?"

"She's Taiwanese. Doesn't speak any English. I'd have to spend the whole time translating, which is annoying. Better to show up and get drunk by myself."

"How does she get by?"

"Well, she speaks about five words, or something. She can buy groceries. And order a coffee. But keeping up with our conversations is a pain for her."

"How do you communicate?"

"We don't."

Lazlo raised an eyebrow.

Rock smiled. "I speak Mandarin. Badly."

"I see."

Rock finished the last of a glass of wine he was carrying and decided he wanted to take a piss. He handed his glass to one of the caterers, grabbed another and downed it, leaving the empty on the buffet table.

He walked around front and headed inside. So this was the place where Orson Welles died, he thought. Out of morbid curiosity, Rock wandered into the front. This was where he kept his bedroom. Right by the door. Died with a typewriter on his chest. Writing until the end.

Rock went upstairs, looking for the bathroom. He passed by some bedrooms. He heard water running behind one of the doors. Then some moaning. He waited. The moaning stopped. Then snorting. Voices. A man and a woman. The water stopped.

The door opened. Simpson and Samantha emerged.

Rock almost blew a gasket.

They'd been using Ira's bathroom to screw and do lines!

"Oh, hey," said Simpson. "Look, I'm really sorry about your situation. I can't imagine—"

Rock reached in and grabbed his throat. Simpson was as light as a rag doll. Rock tossed him back. Simpson landed on his feet, but toppled backwards into the tub. Rock, anger beating through him, pushed Samantha

169

aside. He grabbed the heaviest thing he could find. The lid to the toilet basin.

He flung the lid down—

—and stopped inches from Simpson's skull. "The only reason you won't spend tonight in a hospital is because I respect any room where Orson Welles once took a shit. I wouldn't want your blood to besmirch its atmosphere of respectability." Rock leaned down, got right in his face. "I don't want you to ever talk to me again." He turned to Samantha. "I have no idea what's going through your head, but I don't want to see you, either."

Rock put the lid back in its place. "I hope you enjoy seeing my children and wife suffer. And my wife's family. Personally, I don't give a shit. I'm used to being humiliated in public. But they aren't. So I hope you feel proud." Rock reached into his sports jacket and pulled out a small slender canister. "Thank you for the mace." He handed it to her.

"Keep it," she said.

Simpson got up. "I'm really—"

"Get out of here. I need to piss."

After he finished his business, Rock headed back outside. Even more people had arrived. Ira was standing up in the boxing ring, next to a referee and two guys. Both of whom, in Rock's opinion, looked like meatheads. Aging meatheads. Ira was mumbling into the microphone, bellowing platitudes to his old company. Rock found one of the caterers and grabbed two glasses of white wine, downing one on the spot. Then sidled up to Lazlo. "What is all this?" he said.

"He found these guys at Gold's Gym in Venice. You know all those actors who used to do those superhero movies?"

"My predecessors?"

"Kinda. They're running out of money now, so they started this backyard-fighting league. It's all a fix. But Ira has it so that people can bet on it. Except he knows who will win, I guess."

"And remember," bellowed Ira through the microphone, "it's no rules, because this is my backyard. Top prize is a quarter of a million dollars. All on me."

Lazlo shook his head. "He'll make ten times that from the bookies. Watch all the junior agents glued to their phones during the match. They get a cut, too."

"And the guys getting their heads kicked in?"

"They're getting some sort of appearance fee."

"I want one of those."

"If you're willing to spill a pint of blood up there. I went to one of these last year in Alhambra. One of the guys was losing, so he got a friend to shoot his opponent. In the middle of the match. But those are mostly Mexican gangbangers. The guys up here are much more respectable."

Rock couldn't decide what was worse. The fact that he didn't care for fights. Or the fact he wasn't the center of attention. He drank some more booze, then left.

Turning onto Hollywood Boulevard, he didn't notice the men in the Mercedes watching him.

38

"Why did you recommend this clinic if we couldn't afford it?"

Doug was speeding down Franklin. He had just turned off the 101, and was fearful of accidents. He always felt Franklin was less prone to car crashes than Hollywood Boulevard.

"I wanted to make you feel better. If I'd known what it was going to cost, I would have bought you some ice cream."

The wind blew through Vivian's hair. Doug had been insistent on leaving the convertible's top down. "Well, what do you want me to do?"

"We just bought a house. And then there's the two cars."

"Why don't you buy a Volkswagen?"

"And then there's the cost of taking care of Finnegan."

"Stop right there." Vivian felt her blood getting ready to boil. "You want me to choose between my dog and my wrinkles? The man on his way to the most expensive golf course in the city?"

"We have a very small yard," said Doug. "I think it's cruel to him. Besides, I need that golf membership. To make connections with agents and managers. How else am I going to set up interviews?"

"They have publicists for that."

"Look, somebody has to convince these people to show up at six in the morning. That's not easy. They see me as a friendly face."

"Then why don't you get Ray to pay for your golf membership?"

"I've asked. He's still thinking about it." They stopped at a red light. "Besides, we both know Finnegan hates it at the new house. He's getting older. Maybe we should—"

"Pull over. I'm getting out."

"What?"

"I've had enough of your bullshit."

"Now wait—"

The light turned green.

"I will jump out of this car," said Vivian, "if you don't pull over."

Doug shook his head, but complied. "How are you going to get home?"

"Who knows? Maybe I'll hitchhike. Or take the subway. All to save money for your designer golf clubs." She reached in the back seat and grabbed Finnegan's leash. "We're going to the dog park. Why don't you think about our marriage during your golf game?"

She slammed the door on her way out.

"We have to make choices," he said, watching her leave.

"Go away! I hate you."

Doug rolled his eyes. Did a u-turn towards La Brea. And drove off.

Vivian turned a corner and headed up the hill towards the dog park. Just in sight of the gate she saw a hideously-faced man with steroid-style muscles walking across the street. He went out of his way to get closer to her. He had a pit bull on a leash that started yapping aggressively at Finnegan. The two dogs were almost at each other's throats.

"Hey, lady, do something about your mutt."

Vivian ignored the guy, pulling Finnegan away.

"It's not my problem your dog's a creep," he said.

She refused to make eye contact. That might give the man some satisfaction. "Come on," she said to Finnegan, pulling on his leash. This guy was a douche.

Vivian moved away and passed through the small narrow gate. They'd moved the offleash area, once again. Farther up the hill.

It was completely deserted. Due to the pit bull, no doubt. Well, maybe the douche had some benefits.

39

Hollywood Boulevard was a strip of low-rise apartment buildings and fast moving traffic. Rock was still far enough from the station that it would be a bit of a hike. Hopefully no more than twenty minutes east of Ira's place. Ira and Shelly drove everywhere. They had no reason to take the subway. Ever.

Across the road the four Nicaraguans sat in their Mercedes. In the sunlight it was clear the bullet holes, patched with filler, had been coated with the wrong tone of paint. In the back seat one of the men unhooked a charger attached to a device that looked like a large egg. With a coil on one end. And a pistol grip on the bottom. It was a magnetic monopole pulse weapon. Better than a gun. But very expensive. Obtained from a weapons dealer in Simi Valley. They needed Rock alive if they wanted to get their water back.

The driver put the car in gear. The road was clear of traffic. The Mercedes followed slowly behind Rock.

Looking around, Rock saw the vehicle. Immediately thought it was sketchy. People in Los Angeles slow down for absolutely nothing. Except a driveby. All four men were staring at him. He broke into a jog. As he reached the curb he heard tires squealing.

The Mercedes cut him off. Three men jumped out. Surrounded him. Rock fought as hard as he could. Elbowed the man on the right, then the man to right of the first guy. Both in the stomach. He kicked the third man in the shins.

Rock ran forward. Was cut off by bushy eyebrows. The man threw him up against the hood of the car.

Then Rock remembered the pepper spray.

From Simpson.

He reached into his jacket pocket. Pulled it out and sprayed bushy eyebrow's face. The man howled in agony. Rock turned around and sprayed the three other Nicaraguans, too.

Then he ran.

40

Rock raced through the side streets. Maybe he could hide down an alleyway. But this wasn't a neighborhood he knew well. He paused at the top of a leafy cul-de-sac. Nothing but gated driveways.

A few years ago he'd taken a course in how to escape a kidnapper. The number one rule was get to a public place. Failing that, find an area where cars can't go. That evens the chase. On foot you might outrun them. Also, while they're pursuing you, there's a chance you can hide. Farther away from the road is better.

Access to the hills above the houses was blocked by a large gate. But Rock found a small passage for pedestrians to pass through. Perfect. They couldn't chase him through there.

Rock headed up the hill. He searched for his telephone. It was gone. One of his kidnappers must have grabbed it, maybe when he was pinned against the Mercedes. Not good. He had to find someone with a phone.

The park was empty. He climbed around the edge, near a line of trees, when he spotted a woman in the off leash area.

He ran towards her, leaping over the low fence that kept the dogs in. "Hey, you've got to help me—"

The woman turned around. Rock was shocked when he saw it was Vivian.

She was equally surprised. "Are you stalking me?"

"What are you talking about? Are these your friends? Chasing me?"

"Huh?"

"Give me you phone."

"No."

"Then call the police."

"Wait a minute, how come you and I are in the same place? That's not a coincidence."

"Yes it is. Now will you call the cops?"

"Why?"

Rock couldn't believe her stupidity. "There's no time." He grabbed her handbag and unzipped it.

"Get lost, asshole."

Rock rummaged through the bag as Vivian tried to grab it away from him. He found her phone.

"Give me that back," she screamed, trying to rip it out of her hands.

"We've got to get out of here, now," he said, dragging her towards the off-leash gate.

"No way, I've got to get my dog. He needs his leash—"

Rock struggled to find the dial pad on her phone.

Finnegan barked.

"Stop," she said grabbing the phone, "let me do it."

Finnegan was going nuts.

"Now, first, tell me what is going on—" Vivian stopped mid-sentence.

Rock turned around. The four Nicaraguans came over the hill. One had a shotgun. Another, with the pulse cannon, aimed towards them.

Rock saw a flash of blue light and everything went dark. The last thing he remembered was his numb body on the ground. Blue sky. And Vivian crashing on top of him.

The Nicaraguans hopped the fence to the off-leash area. "This is a problem," said bushy eyebrows. "We'll have to take her, too."

41

Darkness. Everything was darkness. This was it, thought Rock. This is me. After death. My eternal afterlife. This is what happens. You're just a floating consciousness. In a void. Forever. A state of purgatory. Everybody ended up this way.

He thought back to all the good things that had happened in his life. All the movie roles. The parties. And the women. All of it had started in a low-budget remake of Play It As It Lays. Directed by a man who was a homicidal maniac. He'd gone on trial, a couple years after they'd made that picture. Who knew the jury would get him for murder one? Yet, in many ways, that first film was able to convey Rock's morbid disappointment with his life. It still haunted him.

Rock felt like that director. Someone who had gotten away with murder. Now it had all caught up to him. He regretted not doing more with the chances he'd been given. Rock would never get to be the director in real life. Not Dougie's movie, or his one artistic dream—a remake of The Old Country Where Rimbaud Died. Never be able to answer the critics in Canada who felt betrayed that he'd become an American movie star. The height of distaste for many up north. He had even taken French lessons.

In the void his consciousness sloshed around like wine in a decanter. Until Rock began to realize it was his stomach. The void began to sound an awful lot like Los Angeles traffic. He felt pressure, like the car was making a right hand turn.

His body didn't quite ache, as much as everything just felt numb. Then his sight came back. Little dots of light poked through the darkness. Oh my god, he thought, I'm not dead. His body was flung to the side. They were heading up a hill. He must be in the back of a car.

Something wasn't right. Something was crushing his balls. He tried to lift it away.

"Hey, stop that." It was Vivian. Her face was in his crotch.

"Would you get your head off my neither regions?"

She shot up and banged against the trunk. "Owwww." She rubbed her head. "Where are we?"

Rock could now discern her face through the pinpricks of light. "In some sort of compartment. Probably in the back of an ancient Mercedes."

"Who are those people? What have they done to us? Why am I talking to you? Are you stalking me?"

"Well, we're both celebrities. Or at least, I am. Maybe they want to hold us for ransom. Like Frank Sinatra Junior, or something like that. This has always been my greatest fear. I've taken a self-defense course, you know."

The car slowed down. The road got bumpier. The sound of pebbles and rocks dinged off the metal exterior.

"You got me into this, didn't you?"

"No. It was all bad timing. A coincidence."

"I don't believe in coincidences."

"It doesn't matter what you believe. That's the truth. I'm surprised more rich people aren't kidnapped in this country. Given the level of income inequality."

"Where's my dog?"

"I have no idea."

"They hit us," said Vivian, "with a stun cannon."

"A what?"

"The L.A.P.D. have two of them. I did a news story on exotic weapons a couple of months ago. The whole thing has been kept a bit hush-hush. They don't know the long-term effects of this technology. It's a magnetic pulse whacking against your nervous system. Knocks you completely unconscious."

"And numbs all your senses?"

"We were lucky we were in the park."

"How?"

"If we'd collapsed on concrete, I could've cut my head open."

"Lovely."

185

"They call them 'Harm-free weapons.' But not if you fall into something on the way down. And they can be deadly to smaller animals."

"Lady, for fuck's sake, let's worry about OUR lives, first."

"You've never had a dog—"

"It's hot in here. I bet they're taking us out to the desert."

The car stopped.

"Looks like it's show time." The gangsters got out of the car. Rock heard angry yelling.

Vivian turned her head to the side. "They're talking in Spanish."

"You know it?"

"A little."

The top of the compartment opened. Vivian and Rock were blinded by sunlight. He saw the silhouette of the man with bushy eyebrows. Rock looked around. They'd been smushed into some sort of packing crate. Like they were about to be mailed. Or something.

Bushy eyebrows smiled. "Now you get out."

"And what happens if we don't?" said Vivian.

The Nicaraguans laughed. Bushy eyebrows responded by raising a shotgun.

42

It was obvious they were somewhere in the Hollywood Hills. Rock just needed to catch a glimpse of the horizon. Which was blocked by bushes and trees. Maybe somebody would walk by. See them and call the police.

The Nicaraguans had tied them to a tree. Together.

"I'm guessing we're somewhere in Griffith Park," said Vivian.

"This place is usually busy."

"It's Friday afternoon. People aren't going hiking at this time of day. They're already on their way home."

Rock looked around. They were near the side of a hill, but just far enough from roads and hiking trails that no one would notice. Much of the area was obscured by foliage.

Bushy eyebrows approached. "We want to know something. Why did you steal our water?"

"I stole nothing."

"We saw you with the Swiss drug dealer."

"Your water?" said Vivian.

"It's complicated." Rock looked up at bushy eyebrows. "I don't know where he gets his stuff."

"What about the Nigerians?"

"I have no idea."

"Perhaps we use you as a bargaining chip."

"Fine," said Rock. "But let the woman go. She was just in the wrong place at the wrong time."

"No," said bushy eyebrows. "She knows our faces. We will let her go once we have our water back and are out of the country."

"Well," said Rock, "what do you plan to do?"

"The man who sold us the water, we think he has betrayed us. Nothing is more important than his privacy. Bringing you here will focus attention on his activities. That is why we had to kidnap you."

One of the Nicaraguans, standing over by the car, made a suggestion. The group moved over to the foliage. Bushy eyebrows yelled back, they argued for a moment, then he joined them behind a shrub.

"What did he say?" asked Rock.

"I don't know," said Vivian. "I didn't take much Spanish in high school. I think one of the men made a suggestion. The man with the bushy eyebrows got angry. Now they're having a conference."

"Thank you for describing the obvious. Did you understand any of the actual words?"

"Hey, look, it might help if you told me what this is all about."

Rock sighed. "I bought some heavy water. But not that much. Not enough for these guys to kidnap me."

"They're obviously desperate. You made yourself a target."

"Yeah."

"And how did you get it? They shut down all the fission reactors in California last year."

"My dealer, the Swiss guy, told me he got it through a bunch of Tibetans. They're building a bomb to take over West China, or something. Or maybe Southeast China. I'm not sure. Anyway, they were trading the water for spare parts. To build a missile delivery system. Or so I'm told. Using rockets from the Maoists in India."

"This is for real?"

"It's a complicated pipeline of different warring factions. They don't have anything else to trade."

A plume of smoke drifted past them. Rock smelled something. "Are they smoking weed?"

"I don't smell anything," said Vivian.

"Your nose is still numb from the phase cannon." Rock shook his head. "What's next? Are they going to leave us here when they get the munchies?"

The man with the bushy eyebrows came over. Very mellow. Pointed his shotgun at Rock and Vivian, who looked up, terrified. "We don't want to go back to jail. If you don't have any answers, we'll have to kill you."

"Wait a minute," said Rock. "You'll get a hefty sum if you ransom me. Killing either of us is not the most financially advantageous—"

A sound like fireworks cracked through the air.

Then bushy eyebrow's forehead exploded. Blood, bone, and brain splattering against the tree above Rock and Vivian.

43

The other Nicaraguans took cover in the bushes as a gun battle erupted. Someone was shooting from up in the hills. Rock thought this was it for them. He moved with Vivian to get cover from the other side of the tree, but the rope was bound too tight.

Surprisingly, none of the bullets came close to them.

More gunshots. Rapid fire. One of the Nicaraguans had a full automatic. He ran out the clip. Still more gunshots came from the hill.

"If they're shooting a machine gun," said Rock, "the cops will be here in five minutes."

One of the other Nicaraguans ran over and grabbed the shotgun bushy eyebrows had held. He got half way to the foliage before turning, cocking the gun, and firing. Two shots into the hillside. He had a box of shells with him. Dropping to his feet, he attempted to reload the weapon.

More fire crackled out from the hill. The man with the shotgun had his body riddled with bullets.

Rock caught something strange out of the corner of his eye. He turned to a gully a few dozen feet from the tree where he and Vivian were tied up. The area was caked with brown dirt. Probably hidden from the Nicaraguans by the incline of the hill. It was a green blob... of something. And it was getting closer.

Rock heard scrunching. Like someone was walking in a garbage bag. The blob stopped in front of them, then kept moving. It was almost perfectly camouflaged with the grass and brush around it. Only visible when it was moving.

The blob moved past them, over to the man with the shotgun. A bullet exploded from the blob, hitting the fallen man point blank in the head.

Rock heard the bag unzipping. The green blob came apart, revealing a middle-aged man in army fatigues. With an assault rifle in his hands. It was Dewey.

"Drop your guns, and get out of here," he said.

There was frantic yelling in Spanish. The two remaining gang members emerged from the bushes.

"I told you never to come back. Why are you here?"

One of the men blurted out an answer.

"Say it in English, goddammit."

The man answered something different, still in Spanish.

"I told you to say it in English."

"He can't," said Vivian. "He says he can barely understand you. They brought us here because they think you know the people who stole their drugs."

Dewey shook his head. "Why would I know anything about that?" Dewey reloaded his weapon. "Get out of here."

The Nicaraguans ran to the Mercedes. The car kicked up a cloud of dust as they took off.

Rock watched them go.

Dewey produced a remote control. Pressed the only button on it.

The vehicle was almost out of sight when it exploded.

Rock was in shock. "How did you—?"

"Pretty good, huh? It seems they didn't notice me plant the bomb under the driver's side."

"You're crazy," said Vivian.

Dewey shook his head. "I told them never to come back here." He turned to Vivian and Rock.

"What is that thing?" said Rock.

"This?" said Dewey, holding up the almost-invisible bag. "Our government has been issuing it to all our agents in the far east. Fighting the Maoists. Gives them an edge. Has an array of micro-cameras that can blend me into the background. Not perfectly. It only camouflages from one angle at a time. But you don't need perfection in a firefight."

Dewey bent forward, taking a good look at Rock and Vivian. "Who the hell are you?"

"They just kidnapped us," said Vivian. "We're innocent bystanders."

Dewey grinned. "I doubt that."

"We'll tell the police you rescued us."

"I think I should kill both of you. No witnesses."

193

Then he leaned down and got right in Rock's face. "Or maybe I won't." He put down his gun. "I know you."

"Everyone knows him," said Vivian. "He's a famous movie star."

Dewey shook his head. "From Japan. You were friends with Randy Campbell."

"I had drinks with him a couple times. That's all."

"You got old."

Rock tried to place Dewey's face. It took a moment before it clicked. "You lived in Akita."

"No, I lived in Tokyo. But—"

"The two day march. In Akita. On the coast."

Dewey nodded. "You know my name."

"Yes," said Rock. "We met at an izakaya in Kokubunji." Rock looked at his fatigues. "I didn't know you went into the army."

"You two know each other?" said Vivian.

"Be quiet," said Rock.

"Yes," said Dewey. He examined Vivian's face. "You're the girl who does the morning traffic reports."

Vivian nodded.

"If I killed you two, they might trace it back to me."

"Definitely," said Rock.

Dewey stood up. "It seems this is your lucky day. I'm going to spare your lives. For the time being."

44

Dewey had tied them up with rope. Then blindfolded them. Trudged along a road, past the smoking wreck of the Mercedes. After what felt like an eternity they reached a concrete surface.

Dewey led them up the loading dock, and all the way down into the mineshaft. To the old railway for the mine. He made sure they were securely handcuffed to the manual pump handcar. "Keep your feet in," he said. "You don't want to get hurt."

Rock's ass started to hurt from the hard surface. The mine was hot, muggy, and it smelled bad.

Dewey pumped the lever that set the handcar in motion. About a mile down the track when arrived at an area that had been dug out of the wall. A huge conveyor belt, illuminated by bright lights. The belt was wide enough to accommodate the device that had been smuggled out of the air force base. At the end of the conveyor was a giant hole, capped by a large metal grate. The grate, in turn, was attached to a hydraulic arm. At one end was a workstation. With numerous control panels of buttons, knobs and flashing lights. And a bank of monitors above them, displaying technical readouts.

Dewey undid Rock and Vivian's blindfolds. "Right here," he said. "This is where all the action is going to happen."

"What?" said Rock. "Are you a prospector? Did you strike it rich?"

"Don't mock me. I'm giving you a fighting chance for survival." Dewey looked around. "Of course, once all this shit goes down, you might be dead of dehydration."

"If you just undid our restraints," said Vivian, "maybe we could talk this out."

"I'd love to," said Dewey. "But I have to go."

"Huh?" said Rock. "Where?"

"Away from here. Need a good spot to watch all the fireworks."

Dewey walked away, back towards the elevator.

"Stop! You're leaving us to die!" yelled Rock. "We're handcuffed."

Dewey tossed a set of keys towards Rock. They bounced off the handcar. Landing near one of the rail ties. "Too bad I'm a terrible shot." Dewey turned around. "Gotta go now."

"You're just letting us escape?"

"By the time you get out of those cuffs, no one will care about what happened to you."

45

"The man is clearly completely insane," said Rock.

"What is that thing, on the conveyor belt?" asked Vivian.

"No idea."

Vivian reached over. "Maybe I can unlock the handcar." She strained her legs to move the brake. With all her leg strength she got it between her feet, and pulled it towards her. The mechanism creaked and groaned.

The handcar came loose and began to move. The wrong way.

"Wait," said Rock, "hit the brakes."

Vivian leaned back, complying. They slowed.

"I'll use my feet to push us toward the keys."

"Hurry up. My legs are in pain."

Once again, Vivian loosened the brake. Rock pushed

against the loose gravel. His other foot lodged in the rail ties. It was awkward, but they moved forward, right next to the keys.

"Hit the brakes," he said.

"Grab the keys."

"I can't."

"Well, take your shoes off."

Rock kicked off his loafers and socks. Like a monkey he grabbed the small metal keychain between his toes. He reached down, trying to grab them from his foot with his jaw. But he wasn't flexible enough.

Vivian was watching all this play out. "You have to toss them towards my hands. I'll unlock you."

"You mean kick them towards you? And what if they go wide?"

"We have no choice. Toss it with your feet and get it right. One chance."

Rock focused on his toes. Like he was stamping the air, he tossed the keys toward the center of the handcar.

They landed right in Vivian's hands. "Perfect." She got to work fingering for the lock. "You should play in the NBA."

It took some time, but she managed to unlock Rock's handcuffs. "Thank god," he said rubbing his red-marked wrists. He unlocked Vivian.

The two stood up, examining the cavern in front of them. Rock looked at the hydraulic arm, attached to the sewer grate. "It's like it comes up, and the conveyor belt drops that device in the hole."

"And it goes where?"

"No idea," he said. "This is so bizarre." Rock looked up at one of the monitors. "There's a countdown going on." It had forty-five minutes to go.

Vivian examined the schematics. "It's like he's drilling for something. Oil?"

Rock shook his head. "I don't know. This looks like an old gold mine. Either way, we've got to find a way out of here."

Vivian massaged the soles of her feet. "I lost my flip-flops."

"Here, you can take my shoes."

"No, it's okay—"

"Look, I've got socks on. I don't want to give you my shoes, but I'm doing it because it could be a long walk out of here. And I feel bad for getting you involved with this. If you prefer to go barefoot—"

"Give me the shoes." Putting them on, she found a tablet computer on a shelf under the control panel. "What is this?"

"No idea. Take it with you. It might be valuable. Let's get the hand car moving."

With Rock pumping and Vivian on the brake, they went all the way back to the mineshaft that connected to the elevator. They trudged for ten minutes, only to find the lift was non-operational.

"Does that tablet do anything?" asked Rock.

"There's a password on it."

Rock took the tablet and pushed it up against the elevator button. "Some of these things are radio controlled."

Nothing happened.

Vivian took the pad from Rock. She turned it off, then back on again. The display appeared, without a pass code.

"How did you do that?"

"People forget to set a password for when they turn it on. The login is just to discourage people from snooping." Vivian found something. "Look."

Rock peered over her shoulder. It was some sort of blueprint. For a building.

"He has a whole complex here. This is the mine. It leads somewhere, maybe an exit." A dot pulsed on the screen. "This is where we are. It looks like the mine goes for miles. Deep into the mountain."

"What's that space on the side of the shaft? It says 'drill bore.'"

Vivian zoomed in. "No idea. I didn't see a drill. He must be digging for oil."

Rock took the tablet from her. "We're right under the Hollywood Hills. Do you have your phone?"

"No. It's in my purse. Probably back at the dog park." She examined the schematic. "Let's head to the top of the mine. Maybe we'll find an exit."

They headed back to the handcar, riding it to the top of the shaft. All the pumping exhausted Rock. The rails ended at a giant steel door. "It has no handle," he said.

Vivian held the tablet against the entrance. Nothing happened. She ran the device along the smooth contour of the metal. There was a heavy clinking. The door sprung open. Rock grabbed the metal edge that had been revealed and pulled. Behind was a set of stairs.

Above them, Rock heard a fan turn on. "Obviously there's power and air conditioning. It's like he left us access to everything. If we were smart enough to escape from the handcuffs. Why would he do that?"

"Because he doesn't want to kill us," said Vivian. "He feels bad that we've been victimized by his actions. By that gang."

"You must be joking."

"Seriously. Whoever he thinks is his enemy, it's not us. And he made sure he had plenty of time to get away. How long is the drive to the Mexican border? He's probably half-way there."

"But he's crazy."

"Not that crazy. Obviously he doesn't want to kill everyone in sight. Only those he thinks wronged him."

Rock started up the stairs. "Who knows? This is the most bizarre thing that's ever happened to me."

At the top of the stairs was another heavy door, this one with a handle. It was unlocked.

It led to Dewey's giant underground abode.

"Look at this place," said Rock. "It's like Frank Lloyd Wright built a fallout shelter."

"Or a burial tomb."

But Vivian had to admit, the room was stunning. Polished marble floors. Modernist furniture. Intricate wood paneling interspersed with rock walls.

"It's beautiful," said Rock.

"I don't know. It looks like the kind of place a movie villain would live. I don't think it has a single outside window."

"Um, well, yeah. I guess it's a bunker." Rock found a wall panel with light switches. Flicking them on revealed other rooms in the complex. They were in a giant foyer. It led to a large open living room, bordered by bookshelves. One end was designated a games room, with pool, billiards, and a ping-pong table. Rock wondered who Dewey would play with down here.

Vivian yelled to him. Rock rushed over. She'd found a long hallway. Paintings adorned the walls.

"This is a Rembrandt. Storm on the Sea of Galilee. It was stolen from the Boston museum almost forty years ago. She glanced at the other paintings. And this one—" she pointed to a canvas with a bucolic scene— "it's a Cezanne stolen from a museum in Oxford. In fact, I'm willing to bet all these paintings are stolen."

"So he's... an art thief?"

The hallway led to a dining room. The walls lined with mannequins, dressed in elaborate military costumes. Each from a different country and era.

"I've done some war movies," said Rock. "Looking at the ranks, I'd say these were all worn by important people." He examined a Nazi uniform in the far corner. "Oh, my god."

"What?"

"If this is real, then it was worn by Adolf Hitler. These are his war medals."

The door at the opposite end led to a giant kitchen.

"Look at this setup," said Vivian. "It must have cost millions."

"No way."

"My husband did a segment for the morning news on luxury kitchens. This could feed an army. If need be. Frank Sinatra had one just like it. Installed in his old house. The kind of thing you might see in a hotel restaurant."

Rock found an alcove with a washer and a dryer. "Well, at least we can do laundry."

They walked to the other side of the main living room. A doorway led to a room decked out like a seaside tavern. With tables for people to sit at. Off it was an office. One wall devoted to a workstation.

"It's like mission control in here," said Rock. The wall was covered with a bank of monitors. Some showed technical displays, other security cameras. With views inside the mine, and of the surrounding hills.

They went back to the foyer, leading to yet another hallway. At the end they found three bedrooms, each with an ensuite bath.

"I don't understand," said Vivian. "Does someone come in here and clean it out every day? They must. You could never do it by yourself. And there's no dust on anything. He must have a maid staff."

Back in the kitchen they examined the contents of the fridge. "Look at this," she said, "it's like everything is catered. And fresh, too. He just stocked up."

"Like he was expecting an extended stay here," said Rock. He had found another side room, devoted to wine. "And you think no one noticed the stolen art?"

"How much do most Mexican housekeepers know about impressionist paintings?"

"You never know."

"But there's no way to get out of here."

An alarm sounded. Every digital display in the house began to flash. A countdown, from one minute. "What the hell is that?" said Rock.

They ran to the office off the bar. The monitors were all going crazy. It was clear something was going to happen. Something bad.

Vivian found a monitor that received broadcast television. She turned on the local news channel. "Nothing's happening."

"Look at this," said Rock. "It's a satellite. Moving into position over Southern California. Over us."

Vivian clutched him. "What if we're going to die?"

The countdown changed to single digits.

"Get under the desk."

They crouched down, pulling themselves tight together. Rock closed his eyes. Waited for the unthinkable to happen.

But nothing happened. They stayed gripped together for a couple of minutes, then Rock got up. Looked around.

The countdown had finished. "What was it for?"

Vivian stood up, feeling relieved.

Until she saw the television.

46

If you had been on a space station orbiting over Los Angeles at that exact moment, you would have seen the Southern Californian landscape briefly drenched in orange and yellow. Before dissolving into grayish-black.

Closer in, the brief burst of light would appear like a grid. Aligning exactly with the roads and freeways, with great flashes over parking lots. At that moment, every single vehicle, spare a few antiques that were used on movie productions, simultaneously exploded.

Many people were in their back yards. Others were like Ira, who had left after the barbecue finished at his house. He wanted to get in some sailing as the sun went down. At the moment of the explosion he was mopping the deck of his twenty-five foot yacht, moored in Marina del Rey. Seeing the smoke streaming up from the basement garages of the nearby condo buildings, he decided it was a good time to set sail. His wife, sleeping off her drunk in the cabin down below, jolted awake. The flames from nearby vehicles were so bright she thought the marina was on fire.

The explosion started with a huge sonic boom. Followed by a wave of heat. Burning the air.

Doug had been sitting back at the TV station. In Ray's office. Just after their golf game. The two of them were downing scotch. Doug was holding his own. Then the entire building shuddered. At first they thought it was an earthquake. The walls were thick enough to muffle the sound of the explosion. Then came the stench of smoke. From the parking lot.

Doug walked out to the loading door, looking right outside. People were screaming. All the cars were either on fire or unrecognizable balls of metal and plastic. It was fifteen minutes before the five-thirty newscast started. He walked to the center of the lot, only to find both of the news anchors dead, their bodies a mess of blood and shrapnel. They had picked the wrong time to go out for a smoke. Ray ran to tend to them, but it was too late.

Simpson had hunkered down by the pool at the Standard Hotel in West Hollywood. He had been sipping a margarita, looking over the skyline when the explosion happened. He cowered as his body was hit by the sonic wave. People screamed. And jumped in the pool. He thought it was a nuclear bomb. And was shocked when he realized the city, through the smoke, was still there. He looked down on Sunset Boulevard, which was blocked by the smoking carcasses of vehicles as far as the eye could see. Many buildings had smoke billowing out from the ground floor—the floor used for parking.

Dougie had been sitting with a couple of girls and a friend from university in Iowa when the shit went down. The friend had gotten a gig, housesitting at a Hollywood Hills mansion with a view that stretched to the ocean. They panicked when they saw the state of the driveway and the garage. But Dougie, after putting out the flames with a fire extinguisher, had wandered outside, joint in hand, to the patio overlooking the city. He watched the blackness coalesce into a giant plume, almost like a thundercloud. All of the neighbor's cars were on fire. He hoped the place wasn't going to burn down. Fire trucks weren't coming. One of the girls found a telescope. Dougie took a look, turning it to the 101 Freeway, and gasped. It was nothing but a wall of darkness.

Samantha had been on that same freeway, driving north when her car exploded, flinging the hood up towards the windshield. That was all that saved her from the billow of flames and flying debris from other cars. She pulled over to the side of the freeway. Her car was pummeled around as other drivers crashed into her. Even with no working engines, most of the vehicles kept their momentum. The Toyota was bounced around like a bumper car. In the end, though, she wasn't seriously injured. Just bruises. She rolled down her window, crawled out, and ran up the grass embankment. Where she sat, stunned and scared. Covering her ears from the screams of the dying and wounded.

Back in Dewey's bunker, Vivian and Rock flipped through TV stations. Watching replays of the explosion. From traffic helicopters.

"This is a disaster," said Vivian.

Rock looked up at the monitors. "It might get worse."

"How?"

Rock pointed up to the screen. A second countdown had started. T-minus forty-five hours. And counting.

47

While it was dinnertime in Los Angeles, it was already after ten in Cape Breton. Candy had already put the children to bed. Only then did she get a chance to see what was going on in Southern California.

She felt sick watching the images. The sun was going down in Los Angeles, backlighting the fires. Creating eerie images—much of the city was shrouded by smoke mixed with fog, wrecked automobiles burning along the roads. It was like a volcano had erupted.

For the first time in two days, Candy felt her anger replaced by fear. She dialed Rock's phone. Got no answer. That wasn't entirely unexpected. According to the news scroll, almost all phone service in Southern California had gone out.

Candy waited another half hour. Then tried Ira's number. Miraculously the line connected. He spoke quickly, and Candy tried to confirm what little information he had, repeating it back to him. Then he began rambling on, using words she didn't understand. It sounded like he was panicked about his children. She thanked him and ended the call.

Much of the power was going down due to the destroyed transmission lines. Nothing more could be done on Candy's end. Yet she kept the news on. Watching the endless helicopter shots, and the rambling anchors, much of which she couldn't understand.

Her worst fears were always that a major earthquake would strike while Rock was in California. Or that he would be killed in a landslide. Or a wildfire. That was part of the reason she refused to live there. One of the things she liked about the east coast was that it was seismically stable. Despite the wretched springtime weather.

She didn't want her children to lose their father. After convincing herself she had to leave him, she couldn't bear to be ripped apart like this.

Candy fell asleep that night with the phone in her hand, waiting for his call.

48

Rock and Vivian were shell-shocked. In Dewey's bunker, you wouldn't know anything had happened. The TV cameras couldn't help but catch all the dead bodies that were lying around, many thrown from cars as they crashed. An expert had given an interview estimating as many as one in five people in the Southland had died.

"And I'm not even there," said Vivian. The irony was not lost on her that the most popular traffic reporter in the world, according to Doug, was missing the most important traffic story ever.

Rock looked up from the computer. "The internet says they've shut down all the trains. They think it's a terrorist threat."

"Can you get email?"

"No. I can receive data, but I can't transmit typed messages. Or log in to any site."

Vivian turned back to the television. The local stations were playing a loop of the event, images captured from drones, helicopters, and overhead satellites. It was like a nuclear bomb went off, the city becoming a grid of fire. Vivian changed the channel and found Doug manning the news desk. He was doing a pretty good job as an anchor. She felt bad for questioning his masculinity earlier. He was probably doing this thinking she was dead.

Doug introduced clips of a congressman from Bakersfield. A real redneck right-winger. He rambled about eco-terrorists. "It had to be someone anti-car. Anti-freedom. All these new subways have empowered these people."

Rock leaned over and shut off the TV. "Once they bring on the politicians, I can't stand watching."

"I had no idea so many people cared about Southern California." Vivian turned to Rock. "There's no way to transmit out of here?"

"I've tried every trick I know."

"Well, we've got to find another exit."

They spent the next two hours searching the bunker. Pressing buttons. Checking every door. Looking behind furniture and bookcases. Nothing. They went back into the mine, rode the handcar for almost an hour. But the deeper they got, the hotter the air temperature. When it became unbearable, they turned back.

"There has to be a front door."

"That elevator WAS the door."

"No, I don't believe it. What if the mine collapsed in an earthquake? He must have an emergency exit."

They looked around, but found nothing. It was a long grueling journey back to the complex. They looked through the office. Rock was nervous. He kept expecting Dewey to show up at any moment. Then there was the countdown. Only forty-one hours to go. Until what?

"We're not that far from people. We must be under Griffith Park."

"How do you know for sure?"

"The time. I checked it when we got back. That gang didn't take us that far. We'll just have to wait until someone finds us. The cleaning staff. Or the cooks. Things can't get any worse."

Vivian gazed at him. "And that other countdown?"

"I don't know. But my brain is fried. We need sleep."

49

Rock woke up in darkness. As his eyes adjusted, he saw the glow of the light panel on the wall. He walked over and turned them on. He'd spent the night on one of the couches, a comfortable leather sofa of possible Italian origin. He wanted to be the first person Dewey encountered. Should he have decided to return. It might give Vivian a small chance to slip out undetected.

He wandered to Dewey's office. Turned on the monitors. Rock checked the clock. It was half past one in the afternoon. In the total darkness he'd overslept. Sixteen hours straight.

Heading to the other end of the bunker, he knocked on Vivian's door. After several tries, he entered, walking into a pitch-black room. Hit the lights. Walking over to the bed, he shook her awake.

She had kicked off the bed sheets while tossing and

turning in the night. He tried to suppress his delight that she was dressed in nothing more than her bra and panties. When shaking her had no effect, he tickled her stomach.

Giggling, she fought him off.

"Get up," he said, pushing her hands away from him. "We need to get out of here."

"Fine, go make me coffee."

"What do you think this is? The Peninsula Hotel?"

"The decor matches."

Rock went to the kitchen. He found coffee, and even fresh cream. Dewey had stocked up recently.

Vivian appeared a couple of minutes later. "How do you know that coffee isn't poisoned?"

"Why go to such trouble when he could have shot us?"

She grabbed a mug. Rock was surprised she had found a bathrobe that fit perfectly. Vivian noticed Rock's eyes on her. "I found it in the closet, near the bathroom. With freshly laundered towels and bath salts."

Rock grabbed some oranges from the fridge and began peeling.

"You need to wash those clothes," she said.

"Why? It's not like I have anywhere to go."

Vivian took her coffee to the office. On KXXX she saw Cindy doing coverage. There was a massive operation going on to clear the road to Northern California. They were starting in Lancaster and moving south. Tow trucks had arrived from four states already. Necessary medical and food supplies were being transferred by subway and train, both closed to commuters until next week. The phone system was only working sporadically.

On the internet, people were already posting links of burned out cars and destroyed garages. Someone had taken all the photos and built a map of the worst hit areas. Which was South Los Angeles and Long Beach. Winds from the Pacific had fanned the flames. Vivian thought they were lucky the whole city didn't burn down. She checked her own neighborhood. Doug hadn't posted any photos, but it seemed less damaged than other places.

On the television, an expert was suggesting the only thing keeping the level of destruction down was all the electric cars. If they had been gasoline-powered, they would have burned much longer.

Vivian left, headed back to the kitchen. Looking again in every corner for a secret passageway. And found nothing.

She left her mug in the kitchen. A shower was what she needed to clear her head.

In the bedroom, she saw Rock had gotten there ahead of her. He had stripped down to a towel, and was shaving. She stood there, just watching him. He hadn't noticed her. The thought put a smile on her face. She admired his rather muscular physique. Pretty good for a man who was over forty.

The towel around his waist slipped. Vivian got a good look at Rock's unadulterated body. He splashed his face. Vivian giggled in embarrassment. Rock turned to pick up the towel. Saw her standing there. He rolled his eyes and shut the door to the bathroom.

She waited in the bedroom for him to finish. He emerged with his clothing. "Have you tried to use the washing machine?"

"No," she said, heading for the shower. "Hope it's not poisoned."

Rock headed to the laundry room. Mused about how this crisis had been reduced to domestic chores. But he had no idea what else to do. He'd done plenty of background on prisoner of war camps in World War Two, and the only thing that kept many soldiers sane was a regular schedule of chores and tasks. It was the only thing they could do to keep their dignity. While they waited for the war to end. Or rescue.

Rock hit the button to start the washer. A moment later the bunker was buffeted by waves of violent shaking, like explosions going off. Rock ran to find Vivian, to see if she was all right. He found her cowering in the doorway of the bathroom. Bending down, he wrapped his arms around to comfort her. Both their towels slipped off briefly. They wrapped them back on, and Rock led her to the bed. For a few minutes she just buried her head in his arms.

Finally she calmed down. "What is happening?"

"It was probably just an earthquake. Everything's fine. It's safer to be underground, you know."

"That's hard to believe."

"I'll bet the shaking was way worse up above. That's why I refuse to live in tall buildings."

"What if there's an aftershock?"

"Just make sure nothing falls on you. That's were the danger lies. Bookcases, monitors, speakers."

"What if the roof caves in?"

"Hide under a table and hope for the best. But that almost never happens. In developed countries, anyway. And it's completely out of your control." He stroked her hair. "Tell me what you're afraid of."

"I don't know... it's all very..."

"Did you read about me? Recently?"

Vivian nodded. "You got caught having an affair."

"So life's a lot worse for me, than for you. And I'm not panicked. Do you have children?"

"I have a dog. I might want a child someday."

"Right now everyone is suffering. But promise me one thing."

"What?"

"No matter what happens, try not to see yourself as a victim."

50

They lay there, cuddling for an hour. Vivian seemed to need it, and Rock was happy to oblige. Her towel fell open briefly, providing Rock with an instant hard-on. She caught the material before it completely slipped off. Tightening it again.

She glanced down and saw his erection. "I have a husband."

"Yeah? And where was he while you stood staring at my naked body in the bathroom?" Rock pushed her away. "You're a goddamn Peeping Tom."

"Don't talk to me like that." Vivian was angry. "I was shocked."

"By what?"

"That you would shave without your clothing on."

Rock stood up, still only clad in a towel. "I'm going to make something to eat."

"What about finding a way out?"

"We will. But I can't figure this out on an empty stomach. We need to find out what he's planning. There's a countdown. We have to figure out what it's for."

"And how are we going to do that?"

"I don't know. But the clues are here. Dewey let us into his plans. Maybe, subconsciously, he wants us to stop him."

"He's gone to all this trouble. Why would he want that?"

"Because he's a crazy person. Their thinking doesn't always make sense. When you've got a mental illness, that's the way it goes." Rock leaned in close to her. "Between you and me, something here is amiss. That could be our only way of stopping him. But I can't do that when I have an appetite. Besides, we might die here."

"Don't say that."

Rock stood up. "What do you eat?"

"I'm usually a vegetarian."

"I saw some oranges and pears in the kitchen."

"That's fine."

Rock returned a few minutes later with a plate. "I found strawberries, too."

Vivian was in the bathroom, washing her face. She emerged, toweling off. They both sat down on the bed and attacked the food. Like hungry animals. The tray was bare in minutes.

She lay down on the bed beside him. "This place could end up being our burial tomb. Or he could come back. Walk in on us at any moment."

Rock's gaze drifted down to the sumptuousness of her thighs. Where they met the hem of her towel.

Vivian turned over and buried her face in the pillow. At the same moment Rock caught a brief glance under the fabric she was clad in. It transformed him into a teenage boy again, his body flooded with erotic hormones. She reached around to cover her vagina with the towel. As if she knew what she was doing.

Looking down, Rock noticed he was building a tent.

"We can't do this," he mumbled to himself. "Discipline."

"What?"

He couldn't help it. His leg brushed up against hers. Then he retracted it. Closed his eyes. Felt her leg slide between his. His body became a rush of erotic excitement. He leaned over and began to kiss her naked thighs.

"Stop. Go away. I have a husband."

"You're right," he said, turning away. "And I have a wife. This is wrong. It's what's destroying my marriage. My lust for other women. The last thing I should do is involve you in my life."

"It's okay," she said, rubbing the side of his abdomen.

He moved her hand away. "No. We can't." He turned over. Nothing happened for a moment. The he felt her legs again, sliding against his. Her hand undid his towel. Reaching for his cock. She began jerking it. He felt her towel slip away, her nipples hard against his back.

Rock couldn't be stopped. He turned over and kissed her lips deeply. Then her neck. Ripped away his towel.

She began to moan. He moved down and kissed her nipples. Screams of pleasure erupted. He felt the tip of his glans against her labia. Slowly, he pushed it in, coating it with the wetness of her pussy.

Vivian shrieked in pleasure. Grabbed his legs to push him further.

Rock had barely got the tip in. He thrust. Three, maybe four times. Shot his load inside of her. Then collapsed in her arms.

"That was... nice," she said.

He smiled. Kissed her neck. "We're just getting started."

51

Rock awoke to find Vivian already up. A faint glow permeated the hallway outside the room. Along with the scent of cooking.

He rubbed his eyes. Reached over and stabbed at the light panel. He saw Vivian's wedding ring lying on the bedside table. Picked it up and examined it.

Rock was never one for jewelry. Back in Canada, he had never felt any stigma by leaving the ring off. Americans took the whole custom more seriously. Of course, it helped that his wife was Taiwanese, where even fewer men wore their wedding bands. He placed it back on the table. After all the things that had happened to him, he wasn't sure he wanted Vivian to go chasing after his hand in marriage. If he survived, his life would be complicated enough.

After shaving and washing his face, he walked to the kitchen. "What are you making?"

"Spaghetti with garlic, walnuts and broccoli."

"Sounds delicious. But for breakfast?"

"I always try to pack the most calories in at the start of the day. Go to bed hungry."

Rock made coffee, grabbing mugs from the cupboard.

Then he set the table. Vivian came over with two plates of pasta.

"You're making me feel like I'm back in college." He glanced down at her legs under the skimpy bathrobe.

"That's how I feel too." She leaned up and pecked him on the mouth. He pulled her against his body, kissing her long and deep.

She pulled away. "Breakfast will get cold."

He got in a couple more pecks before he let her sit down.

She nuzzled his leg under the table. "This is kind of my fantasy. Being trapped underground. With a movie star all to myself."

"Is your marriage really that boring?"

"Aren't all marriages?"

"I suppose they get that way. What's wrong with your husband?"

"He's a yuppie. Someone with few life goals other than his golf game."

"And you want to have kids? Give him something to drag him back to earth?"

"Maybe."

"That's a terrible thing to tell a man. Be the old ball and chain."

"I don't really want to talk about him right now."

"Sure." Rock chewed on some spaghetti. "We'll survive down here a few more days."

"Unless that guy comes back."

"He's not. Whatever is going to happen, he knows we won't get in the way."

Rock grabbed himself another cup of coffee. "He left us down here with a bunch of supplies. Meaning he didn't plan to take off. That gang ruined all his plans. We ruined them, too. As soon as we get out of here, we'll be caught up in a major manhunt. Looking for him. Our lives will become complicated. You'd better be prepared for that."

"Your life seems to take everyone down with it."

"It does. The risk of celebrity."

There was long pause as Vivian sipped her coffee. "But I would like to know what it would take for you to leave your wife for me."

"I'm not the type who would leave her for anyone."

Vivian shook her head. "I don't believe it."

"What could you do, that a Chinese girl couldn't?"

"I am a Chinese girl."

"You're from California."

"But my family is originally from Beijing. I'm more Chinese than some Taipei migrant."

"Fine, but I can't practice my foreign language skills with you. I paid good money for those classes."

"Why are you so committed to your wife? You publicly cheated on her."

"I might not be the most morally upstanding man,

but I do have a sense of loyalty. I suspect that is why Dewey spared our lives."

"I don't understand."

"Neither do I. But I imagine he sees me as someone of his ilk. He was too chickenshit to kill me with his bare hands."

Vivian finished her spaghetti. "So you think I shouldn't be worried."

"You don't look worried." Rock put down his mug. "We're both treating this like summer camp. And I'll bet so are a lot of the people who watched their cars blown up."

"Those that survived."

"Yeah. We'll all be paying for this time off for a while."

"You think Dewey was responsible for all those cars?"

"I saw the countdown. And I saw the results."

"Maybe it was a coincidence."

"Doubtful."

"Then what is his motivation?"

"Maybe he doesn't like driving."

"He could just take the subway. And what about those Nicaraguans? They got wrapped up in all this. He had no problem killing them. What were they doing for him?"

"Dewey is a drug dealer. The deal went sour. People got shot. It happens all the time."

"No," she said. "Something about this doesn't feel right." She stood up and cleared the table. "We need to find a way out of here. Even if we have to go all the way down that mine."

"There's no one to rescue us. Everything is shut down with the disaster."

"I need to feel like I'm doing something."

"Take a shower. That's what I'm going to do. It'll relax you."

"That's your plan?"

"We're in no position to be rescued. Most of the authorities are out saving other people. If we have to stay down here a week, well, that's the way it is. But someone will find us. At some point, someone will have to come down here to maintain this place. We'll leave then."

"And if your friend comes back to kill us?"

"Listen, he's not my friend. I met him once, twenty years ago. Before he went insane." Rock headed to the door. "And he's not coming back. He's done his act of terrorism."

"What about the thing on that conveyor belt?"

"I'm not a mining engineer. Or an expert on digging equipment."

Vivian slammed her fist down. "You're content to die down here."

Rock turned back to her. "We're both getting out. Alive. But right now we have to accept the reality of the situation. Tomorrow I'll go and explore the mine. But you need to calm down."

Rock stomped into the bedroom, mumbling to himself. What was her plan of action? Dig a tunnel up through the mountain? Send smoke signals? They'd been here less than a day.

Rock unbuttoned his shirt and flung it aside. He heard a small piece of metal bounce off the marble floor.

The shirt had landed on the bedside table, knocking off Vivian's wedding ring. He got down on his hands and knees to look for it. She would be needing it when all this was over.

He flung the shirt back onto the bed. Checked to make sure the ring hadn't been caught in the fabric. Then bent down and ran his hand along the floors. The ring was nowhere in sight, although it could easily have blended into the pattern in the marble.

As he felt under the edge of the box spring, his fingers grazed the metal loop. They also felt something else. A lever. Built into the base of the bed.

Rock grabbed the ring, putting it on the table, then examined the lever. It had no obvious function. Unless the mattress was on a Murphy bed, the kind that folded into the wall. He squeezed the lever, applying pressure upward with his shoulder.

The bed rose, revealing a secret stairway.

At that moment, Vivian stopped in on her way to the washroom. "What is that?" she said, staring.

"I don't know." Rock moved down the stairs. "It's a secret room."

She followed him down. Rock found a light panel, tapped it on. The room was little more than a walk-in closet. Most of it filled with military uniforms. Multiple sizes of combat fatigues. Police uniforms.

Vivian dug through the racks. "He's got costumes for doctors, firemen, paramedics."

"Yeah," said Rock, "his own little wardrobe rental house down here."

They moved further toward the back. At the end, the room got wider, wide enough for two tables and some chairs. On one table markers, pencils, and pens were scattered over a pile of drawings and schematics. More diagrams were pinned to a bulletin board on the wall above. Along with lists of contact info, photos, and schedules.

"I've seen this before," said Rock, picking up one of the schematics, labeled top secret. "This is a nuclear bomb."

Vivian glanced over his shoulder. "It looks like that thing on the conveyor belt."

"It can't be," said Rock.

He turned to the desk on the opposite side of the room. Two ancient CRT-style computer monitors shared a desk with an equally old video monitor, a keyboard, and an old-style mouse. On the floor next to the desk had been placed an ancient tower-style computer body. Rock hadn't seen anything like it in years. He leaned in closer to examine the unit, an old Macintosh machine, plated with turquoise-colored plastic.

"This model is a Power Mac. A G3, I believe." He turned it on, the machine coming alive with its characteristic chord. Rock noted its speakers were hooked up to a mixer and two tape decks. "That's a VCR, and on top of it is an old DVCAM deck."

"I know," said Vivian, "we have a couple around the studio."

The operating system powered up. "OS 8.6? My god," said Rock, "everything here dates from the turn of the century. And yet it all works perfectly."

"I've seen one of these before. When I was a kid."

Rock opened a metal cabinet next to the table. Inside he found lights. Kino-flos. And lots of cable. Sound equipment. On the top shelf he found an old camera. "This is a Canon GL-1."

"So?"

"The first affordable three chip camera."

"Huh?"

"It's not important. I just think it's eerie. Everything here is dated from exactly 1999. Like it's been freeze dried."

"Maybe it works for him."

"It was the first camera I ever made a movie on." Rock moved back to the computer. He checked the menu to see what programs Dewey had been using. "Edit DV? My god. That program hasn't been in use since 2000." He launched the application. A timeline loaded. But it was blank.

"What about all these?" Vivian had found some small DV tapes.

Rock turned on the TV monitor. Inserted a cassette. "Just raw footage. Shots of Los Angeles." Rock hit a button on the computer, scrolled through Dewey's recent projects. Opened one called 'Manifesto. Rough Cut.'

Rock examined it. "It's a movie." He set the cursor to the opening frame. "It's not very long. Let's take a look at it." He hit the spacebar and the movie began.

52

The main titles were like a PBS special on politics from the 1970's. Triumphant marching band music. Over a montage of historical photographs.

"Here we find the American dream," narrated Dewey's voice. "The American Empire. What you are watching is the manifesto of Dewey Lane. Some of you will call me an antichrist. Others will call me a savior. I only humbly bequeath you my intentions. From here, you, the viewer, shall stand in judgment of me."

Vivian looked over at Rock, raising her eyebrows in a what-the-fuck-is-this? gesture.

Up came a map of Asia. "For far too long the United States has been secretly assisting the Eastern Chinese in their attempt to occupy Maoist West China. As a citizen, I do not approve of the use of my tax dollars in this way. I am an officer of the United States Military, sworn to protect my country. Unfortunately, I have been doing anything but. With this in mind, I have taken drastic action. In an attempt to defend the nation in a way that our leadership has failed to do."

The image zoomed in on the map of China. Then dissolved into a map from twenty years prior, when the mainland had been a single unified country. "Before the partition of the People's Republic of China, this nation went from an experiment in capitalist prosperity, to a splintering of factions and pseudo-countries. With an economy firmly controlled by Shanghai. To the deficit of Beijing."

A montage of images flashed through the screen. The effects had been done quite shoddily, probably with this most basic editing software. But the message was clear—a photomontage of the growth of modern China. He must have spent a lot of time on this, thought Rock, even though it looks like shit.

"Now the Chinese sub-continent has splintered into six different nations, divided up along linguistic lines."

The photos changed to shrines. And other religious buildings. "Tibet, formerly subjugated by the Han Chinese, has shed the mask of honor and discipline. To harbor Islamic extremists, and other religious funda-mentalists, looking for a place of refuge. A place where we see the last vestiges of twentieth century weapons. Used to kill vast numbers of people. And who is their number one sponsor? The right wing of American politics. Continuing the western front in the war against Maoist China."

234

The photos dissolved into a map, with an amateur-ishly animated line moving across it. "Then, against the backdrop of Changsha and the great silk road, we arrive at Maoist West China. A puppet state of the Soviet Union. Here the communists are busy raising armies on the propaganda of pseudo-Marxist totalitarianism. While their machines dig to exploit every last seam of coal and valuable minerals. Contributing to international communism's war effort. Why? Because we Americans have supported their enemies." The map cut to photos of the scarred landscape. Rock recognized some of it as Outer Mongolia and Xi'an. Places he'd visited many years ago. "And as the western Chinese decimate their environment, massive amounts of water are diverted from the Yellow and Yangtze rivers. Slowly turning the entire land mass to desert."

Images of cities and buildings flashed on the screen. "Things are no better in the east," continued Dewey. "Shanghai. The world's gun factory. Producing artillery and submarines for a planet secretly at war. Our American tax dollars have gone to build the giant naval base at Zhoushan." A map appeared on the screen, with animated arrows, like an old World War Two documentary. "Creating a shield between the Indian and Chinese sub-continents. With our navies controlling the Pacific Ocean, Shanghai is a beachhead of American Imperialism. Grouped with Korea, Japan, the Philippines, British Malaya, and Taiwan. Protecting them from the incursions of war-torn China."

1980 "The Year The Past Disappeared"

The maps gave way to what looked like clips of a corporate video. "In the south, Macao and the rest of the Canton have become the gambling and Ponzi scheme capital of the world. Formerly the domain of the Swiss and the Caymans, the Canton is little more than a dumping ground for investment products, with Macao as its pleasure palace. A harbor filled with fly-by-night finance companies, set up on boats. How much money has the average person lost since the United States abandoned its social security system? How long before we are all made destitute by a market collapse? All supported, in secret, by the Soviets. And their third-world client states, whose leaders embezzle from their people."

The clips of tall buildings dissolved into rice fields and helicopter shots of smaller cities. "From the Canton, you need not go far to reach the Eastern provinces of Wuhan and Fujian. To find what has become the Frankenstein lab of our modern world. Providing unregulated pharmaceuticals and molecularly modified foods, designed for processing. The breadbasket of an amoeba overgrowing the planet. Predicted, by many reputable scientists, to turn humans into a race of cannibals. As all foodstuffs become derived from the same cellular matter. Will the Irish potato famine strike again? This time a worldwide crisis?"

There was a gap in the timeline.

"He's got quite the set of opinions," said Vivian.

Rock scratched his chin. "I'd believe the part about the Soviet Union."

Dewey's voice continued. "This is a record, a time capsule, of my time. So that people of the future will understand my actions. I expect no sympathy, only recognition, so that these problems will not be repeated."

Another gap. Then images of factories appeared onscreen. "But in Taiwan, the future is truly at war with the human race. Developing killer robots to fight our battles for us. Ready to leave a path of destruction in their midst."

The screen went blank again. The end of the timeline. Rock searched around and found another project called 'manifesto2.' He hit play.

"Finally we come to China proper," said Dewey. "The last kingdom of Beijing, in the middle, nearly surrounded by enemies. Most of its territory siphoned off, it has returned to its roots as a totalitarian state, busy murdering many of its own citizens. The masses enslaved in labors to support the privileged few. The Manchurian provinces a living example of what happens to a society when humanity abandons its shell of morality." The black screen changed to shots of worker camps. "How many people are enslaved? How much damage will be done to the environment before the people rise up, like they did just a few years ago, once again in revolution? It is time the American government allowed this state to collapse on its own, just as it was over the border to the east. Rather than supporting it directly in its fight against West China. Remaining quiet as Beijing suppresses dissenting voices."

The images changed to a large map of Asia. "But this is not the only great power to come under siege. India, too, has become a shell of its former self. The great potential lost in a mire of corruption and conflict. Where before, the leadership feared the divisiveness of religion, now it fears the divisiveness of caste. All partitioned geographically, at war with one another. The fault line between capitalism and communism."

The map zoomed in towards the Himalayas. "On one side stands Maoist East India. Like the Beijing regime, it has attempted to exterminate half its population through famine and polluted drinking water. A eugenic totalitarian society. Sterilizing those who don't support its leadership. A search for racial perfection, destroying its economy. Most of its roads lined with empty fields, littered with decaying livestock and dilapidated dwellings. Erasing entire families from existence."

"North," continued Dewey as the images changed to spectacularly beautiful mountains and valleys, "we have Indian Kashmir. A drug opium paradise with the highest per capita wealth in the world. Where ninety-five per cent of the people are addicted to opium. On a state-sponsored drug plan. Keeping the servant population from rising up."

Another montage, this one of sprawling cities. "To the south, the Democratic Kingdom of Free India. A system copied with near-perfection from totalitarian-capitalist England. With its own all-powerful monarchy. And its own program of eugenics-light— eradicating young women, and eventually its own state, out of existence. A population turning into nothing but men—a worker, warrior class, restless in its futile future. Yet, with such blatant sexism, this is the country most supported by the United States in the Indian Civil War. Depending on its cheap labor to provide goods to the American people. How long before the state has an internal battle on its hands? When so many of the male citizenry finds themselves without wives?"

The screen changed to a map of the United States. "Why shouldn't America be the same? We've become a country of nearly a billion people, barely governable. Led by a power hungry, corrupt government. The bureaucrats at the top have subsumed the role that formerly belonged to the political class. Where politicians are little more than puppets. Content to debate petty grievances and rubber stamp laws. While real policy control has been subsumed by secret military tribunals. And their technocrats—some in Washington, others along the bullet train routes that connect the centers of economic power. Like Roman highways."

Dewey appeared on screen, dressed in his military uniform. "Perhaps it is a flaw of human nature. Once the population of a nation reaches a hundred million people, bureaucrats begin to subsume the powers of elected representatives. And these pithy office clerks are accountable to no one. A process well known to the citizens of Europe, Indonesia, China, Japan, Brazil, Russia and India. The bureaucrats become the enemies of the people, drunk on their own power."

"All of this is the result of the baby boom generation, and their partners in crime, generation X. Neo-conservatives, all of them. Started out with every advantage, they sought to pilfer as much as possible for themselves, denying the less fortunate any place in society. Laying siege to the social contract, so they could get a tax break. All since 1980. No war or depression or trauma of any kind to teach the value of social cohesion." The images changed to those of Russia. "If the Soviets hadn't made the long march back to Moscow, maybe we'd live in a better world. If only Marxism had seen its day." The video ended.

"I'm not following any of this," said Vivian.

"Now I know why he targeted cars. We're the generation that doesn't drive."

"Excuse me?"

"People born before 1980. They're the ones who drive. Mostly."

"I drive."

"But you're rich."

"Okay, but what does this have to do with us? And an abandoned mine?"

"No idea." Rock found another project, labeled 'Los Angeles.' The monitor came alive with footage of the beach, B-roll that could fit anywhere. "The tech companies have colonized our city," began Dewey, "killing the motion picture industry in the process."

This was news to Rock.

"Driven the entertainers to Northern California and Canada. Hyper-capitalists who have no respect for anyone but themselves. They've destroyed our social programs in this country. All under the guise of efficiency and meritocracy. Words they use to conceal the fact that they got lucky. Borrowing from Hollywood an employment model that destroys a worker's right to stability. A permanent lack of a future. What kind of world is that?"

The camera zoomed in on Dewey's face.

"The world that began in 1980. With no future, we also destroy our past. Ever since Reagan was elected. Even if he had survived his assassination, he could never have hoped to see his policies flourish so effectively. All from a presidency that lasted mere months. For baby boomers who saw change as positive and possible. Changing everything by destroying things. Turning against the system that allowed for true meritocracy. Slowly they took away rights and freedoms. The doctrine of Milton Freedman. Turning America into the obese cousin of Latin America. Destroying all collective organization. Now people are free to choose... their own destruction... be it financial, political, emotional, medical, mental. Where markets for guns and biological land mines have flourished. Without a social safety net, it is every man for himself. Not to mention the millions of millennials with liver disease. Nearly thirty-five per cent of all people born since 1980. Because of the amphetamine salts in mental health medications. Willingly doled out by doctors, the lackeys of the pharmaceutical companies."

The film cut to a wide shot of Dewey. In a different uniform. Clearly he didn't care for continuity, thought Rock. "I want to show how the government has abdicated its role. And I will do that by destroying the largest city in the United States—Los Angeles. By killing thirty million people, I will bring together the other billion Americans. The only way to save our country."

The film ended.

Vivian shook her head. "The guy's totally insane."

"Well," said Rock, "he had me until the part where he kills millions of people."

53

They were sleeping when the earthquake hit.

The entire room exploded with the shock wave. That's what it felt like to Rock as everything shook around them. The shaking was mild at first. Vivian had stirred next to him. Then he felt her hands clutching him tightly. The shaking continued, until it ended with a huge boom. In the bathroom he heard a plastic cup fall over.

"What was that?" she said.

"An earthquake, I think."

"What if the mine exploded?"

"No." He caressed her hair.

"You think we're going to get out of here alive?"

"Like I told you before, this is the safest place to be."

They kissed, slowly, then it became deeper.

"You like me?" she asked.

"A lot."

"It's nice to be with you at night."

"You don't mind my snoring?"

"I love it," she lied.

Vivian took off her panties and spread her legs over his naked body, his erection throbbing. She moaned as she rubbed his cock against her, then he reached down and felt her wetness, stuffing himself inside of her. She adjusted herself and began to ride him up and down.

The motions got more and more intense, until her body gripped his in the throes of orgasm. Screaming in pleasure. Half collapsed, she continued rubbing Rock until he came inside of her.

Vivian closed her eyes, burying herself in his neck. "I don't want to leave you. I don't want to leave this space. It's perfect here. Bad things are going on out there."

They cuddled for a while, before Rock got up. "I'm going to check the television. About that earthquake. Why don't you come with me?"

They got dressed. Rock took her hand as they walked to the office. In the long corridor, one of the stolen paintings had come loose.

"Do you see that?" she said.

"No, what?"

"Behind the painting."

Rock stopped as Vivian pulled the frame towards her, revealing a small glass cabinet. Normally obscured by the Rembrandt.

"It's all war medals," she said.

Rock picked up a couple. "They're from China. From battles."

244

"But he's in the U.S. army. We never fought in China."

"No, not officially. Maybe there's something to his crazy rants."

"What? A secret war? How could they keep it a secret in this day and age?"

"I don't know," said Rock, putting the medals back.

They continued down the hall, past the large living room, to the tiny office. Vivian turned on the television. There was Doug, at the anchor desk. The screen was framed by a flashing red bar, something she'd never seen before.

"The rest of the staff is evacuating the station now. With all the traffic, it's going to take time for everyone to get out. The tsunami is expected to make landfall in four hours. We're now switching coverage to our Las Vegas affiliate. Don't pack anything, authorities are saying to get out of your house and get moving now. Trains and subways are running out of the city, and will be doing so until forty-five minutes before landfall. All platforms heading into the city will be closed."

Vivian turned to Rock seated at the computer. "What's happening?"

"That earthquake set off a tsunami out in the Pacific. It's expected to hit southern California. Santa Cruz, all the way to Acapulco, is being evacuated. But Los Angeles and Santa Monica will take the brunt of the destruction."

The television cut to a large map showing the direction of the tidal wave.

"That earthquake," said Rock, "we just felt? It wasn't anywhere near Los Angeles. But some people think it's a new fault line stretching from the far ocean. Hundreds of miles away. The satellite has detected a huge wave. It can be seen from space, even. They think its fifty meters high."

"Which means what?"

"It might destroy the beach at Santa Monica. Or it might take out most of Los Angeles. Nobody knows."

"We've got to get out of here."

Rock turned to her, nonchalant. "Why? We're in the middle of a mountain. We'll be fine." He got up and began to leave.

"What are you doing?"

"I'm going back to bed."

"Excuse me? What if the mine floods?"

"Trust me, we'll be fine."

Vivian was shaking. Rock took her in his arms. "Relax. People are evacuating. We'll only be in the way. We're safe here. Tomorrow I'll find a way out. Climb up the elevator shaft, if need be." He took her hand and pulled her out of the office, towards the bar. "We'll have a drink, and go back to bed."

"And what if Dewey comes back?"

"He won't. His work is done."

"You're just going to bury your head in the sand?"

"It's gotten me this far in life."

54

Dewey was awoken by the roar of traffic. Shortly after sunrise. He had been camped out in the desert for the past three days. He had converted his 1986 Ford F-150 with a camper cab on the back. It gave him enough space for a bed, a hot plate, and bathing facilities. He had parked off a side road, in the desert outside of Lancaster.

The road had little traffic, so it came as quite the shock when the rumble of vehicles started, and didn't stop.

He grabbed the motorbike he'd taken with him and headed to the main road. A young woman was pulled over, changing a flat tire. In her car was an older lady and three kids.

"Can I help you with that?"

"Sure," she said. "I'm terrible with—"

"No problem," said Dewey, getting down on his knees. Traffic roared past, non-stop. "What the hell's going on?"

"You haven't heard? There's a tsunami coming."

Dewey adjusted the spare tire. "Huh?"

"All of Los Angeles and the beach towns are being evacuated."

"I don't have any internet, my truck's too old."

"Yeah, in less than three hours it's going to make landfall. Millions of people on the move."

"Are we safe out here?"

"Probably, but my mother came in from Bakersfield to get me and the kids out. After all the cars exploded. They're running all the trains packed to capacity. People are heading to higher ground. They've switched back the interstate, too. They say it's going to be a forty-meter wave. Could take out half the city."

Dewey finished tightening the spare. "Well, there you go." The woman thanked him, and they took off. Dewey looked at his watch. Just after six in the morning.

He hopped back on the dirt bike and headed back to the truck. Three hours. It would take him at least two to get back to the mine. He might have to kill Rock and the traffic reporter. It wouldn't be difficult hiding their bodies in all the chaos. Finishing the countdown now would be a waste of material. There was no one to kill. The coincidence of it all. Maybe Dewey had caused the earthquake with his attack on the cars. The simultaneous explosions had caused some part of the earth's crust to fracture. Oh, well, he thought. He'd have to be flexible. No main routes. Take the dirt roads through the mountains, enter the mineshaft from the rear entrance. It would take longer. But what choice did he have? He'd have to delay.

Dewey started his truck, turning it towards Los Angeles.

55

Vivian woke Rock up early in the morning. He rubbed his eyes, glancing at the clock. A quarter after six.

He kissed her on the cheek, then moved down to her neck. Her mouth emitted a moan. Quickly he stripped them both naked and ran his hands all over her. In the process Rock decided he really wanted to lick as much of her skin as possible. Like a cat he went at her, discovering each crevice of her form as she cooed in delight, before finally moving his tongue down to the gentle heat between her legs. With one hand he varied his strokes between her stiff nipples, the other assisting his tongue at her clitoris. Vivian's head bobbed up, eyeing him in lost abandon, before flinging back into the pillow, a wave of pleasure overwhelming her. The waves built and built, Rock licked and licked, rubbed and rubbed, until her entire body clenched, a yelp and scream belting out.

When it was over, she pulled him up, laying exhausted in his embrace. Rock felt content with himself. Except for his hard on. He felt her hands dancing around his perineum. Then she leaned down and shoved him inside her mouth, polishing the tip of his head with love and desire, like an animal discovering a miracle of bodily heat. Waves of pleasure rose inside of him. Then she moved around and spread her legs over him. Rubbing his cock against her, then reaching down and thrusting him in. She moaned terrifically, against which Rock could no longer resist. He ejaculated inside of her. She fell down against him, satisfied.

They lie there for several minutes, stroking each other in silence.

Rock looked over at Vivian's forehead. He noticed beads of sweat. It was too warm in here. "Are you hot?"

She looked up at him lazily. "Yeah. It's a lot warmer now."

Rock got up and put on his underwear. Wandered out of the room. When he got to the main open space, he noticed something was different. He walked to the edge of the room. Put his hand over an air duct. The air conditioning was off.

Vivian joined him, turning on more lights. "Is something wrong?"

"I'm worried we might run out of oxygen."

"Maybe it's on a cycle. Come back to bed."

"Maybe," said Rock, although as he took her hand and followed back to the room, he wasn't convinced. They got back in the bed and cuddled. He stroked her hair. "Maybe this should be the last time."

"To do what?"

"Us. Together. I have to go back to my wife at some point."

"And my husband is probably worried about me, too." She kissed his earlobe. "You're very good at this, aren't you?"

"What?"

"Breaking up with women. How do you not feel guilt?"

"I don't know. It's a question that's dogged me my entire life. I just, sort of, get bored."

"With me?"

"Actually, no. You're great. More fun to be with than my wife."

"Maybe you should leave her for me."

"And do what? Spend the rest of my life in Southern California while you read the traffic reports? Take your dog for a walk? How would my children feel? They'd be living halfway across the continent. Or my wife might move back to Taiwan. I'd have to start a whole new life with you." Rock looked over at her. "Were your parents divorced?"

"No. Yours?"

"Still together. Maybe I stay with my wife to avoid making them feel ashamed."

She nuzzled his chest hair. "Maybe that's why generation X destroyed the world. They were all angry at selfish parents. They felt abandoned."

"You've been listening to too much of Dewey's nonsense."

"No," she said, "he's right about the generational angst. We've never been more screwed. More hated by those older than us. And yet, we're much richer than they were. They hate that. It's why they feel the need to govern so oppressively. Dish out some misery to younger people."

"Is that it?" said Rock. "And what happens when they perfect aging therapy? They already cured baldness. Will there ever be such a thing as generations again? We're heading to an old-testament world where we can get away with anything while living for a thousand years."

"That's silliness. People will get bored and die. I'd order a suicide pill."

"Suicide. That would become the natural choice."

"You think?"

"Scientists are reluctant to come out and say this, but humans have a natural limit to the amount of energy they use. After that they stop reproducing. Of course, no one wants to believe that. The researchers and politicians want to believe we're in charge of our destiny. But we aren't. Many species undergo epidemics of cancer or other diseases when they overpopulate. Or they just starve. Yet humans, who have learned to grow far more food than is naturally possible, also reduce their population. Voluntarily. They'd rather get fat than have more children. Because our population has an upper limit of energy consumption on this planet, and it's hardwired into our genetics. Why else would Dewey be doing what he's doing?"

"You're saying his actions are completely natural?"

"Yeah. They're too many humans, and when we over-procreate, nature has ways of limiting us. We don't think of our mental illnesses as ways of culling the population, but they are."

She kissed his arm. "It would explain decreasing fertility. Unless it's all the chemicals in our food. Humans get cancer when they get old. That's a way of limiting the population. I studied Malthus in college. He was completely wrong."

"What was his deal?"

"Basically, he predicted that we'd all starve to death due to overpopulation. Darwin was a big new shiny thing at the time." Vivian shifted in the bed. "Of course, he was proven wrong. But the deeper question, of why the population hasn't exploded now that we can feed people easier, has never been explained."

"The world's population is decreasing."

"Exactly. And no one knows why. If the trend continues there will be no more people in three thousand years."

Rock laughed. "I love predicting the future from trends." He looked at her. "You know a lot."

"I'm not just some dumb broad doing the traffic reports, you know. I have a degree in philosophy. Wrote my thesis on Immanuel Kant." She nuzzled his nose. "Tell me, do you have deep philosophical conversations with your wife?"

"I'm an actor. I don't have deep conversations with anyone."

"Well, next time you blow through town, I'll blow though your underwear. And we can talk our deep thoughts."

"What about your husband?"

"He's too dumb to figure out stuff like that."

"So you wear the pants in your house?"

"Someone's got too."

"We could never be married. You'd tell me what to do. Then I'd walk out." Rock got up and put on a bathrobe he'd found in one of the closets. Mopped the sweat off his brow. "It's goddamn warm in here. We've got to find a way out."

"Why? Because you've discovered you can't handle a smart woman?"

Rock grinned sarcastically. "Exactly. You're learning."

Vivian rolled back on the bed and buried her face in the pillows. She wasn't taking Rock's mock-sexism well. But at the same time, she knew she couldn't have him to herself. Life just didn't seem fair, that's all.

Rock headed to the kitchen. It was when he reached the end of the hallway with the stolen paintings that the smell started. In the main room it hit him—a wall, like rotten eggs, but with a metallic edge.

Gas. The gas was leaking.

He switched on a nearby light. He ran to the kitchen. He inspected the range—and heard a hissing sound. Rock looked around, searching for a valve cutoff. He coughed, and felt nausea building in his stomach. How much longer could he stay here? Every wall was bare of pipes and valves.

He looked through the nearby cupboards. Below and to the right of the stove he found the gas valve. Mounted on the back wall next to a small fire extinguisher. There were other pipes—for hot and cold water, and other things he couldn't identify. With the gas cut off, he searched the drawers for place mats. To use as a fan to clear the air. In one drawer he found candles and barbecue lighters. And behind them, a tablet computer. He grabbed it and searched the next drawer. A Swiss army flashlight with multiple tools, a blade that extended seven inches, with a band to strap it to your wrist. And a first aid kit. Useful items.

Rock switched on the tablet. The first thing to appear were instructions for arming a B83 nuclear bomb. Near identical to the prop papers he'd been given on set by Professor von Stroheim.

Rock flipped through to the end of the document. Checking through the rest of the pad, he found a program called "Thermonuclear Risk Estimator." Tapping it brought up a map program. With giant circles over Los Angeles. Emanating from the Hollywood Hills. Rock zoomed in. The diagram allowed him to look right into the mine, with both overhead and cross section views. He could change the values of the detonation and the wind speed. This had to be Dewey's master plan. The device in the mine was a bomb. It would destroy everything from the ocean to the desert.

Rock zoomed in on Dewey's complex. Saw how it was connected to the mine and the parking garage elevator. Then he examined the complex against a satellite photo of the area.

The far wall of the kitchen faced the outside world.

Rock had an idea.

56

Rock ran into the room. "We've got to go. We have to get dressed."

Vivian rolled over on the bed. "Why? What's going on?"

"I've got a plan. We've got to get this mattress into the bathroom. And take out all the glass in there."

"Why?"

He explained to her about the gas leak and the outside wall in the kitchen. "I'm going to use it to blow us out of here."

"Okay, but maybe we could find better clothes. I need shoes."

They lifted up the bed and headed down to Dewey's secret lair of uniforms. Vivian picked out an air-force jumpsuit. Rock put on a navy uniform. Vivian had no problem finding combat boots that fit. For Rock it was a bit more of a struggle.

He tried tying up a pair of boots designed for pilots. "They're too big. I'll break my ankle."

"Better than sandals."

They found flashlights they could strap to their wrists. Then they went back up to the bathroom and prepared the tub, lining it with as many pillows, duvets, and moving the mattress to cover it. Rock took down the mirror, and pieces of ceramic from the fixtures. Vivian grabbed every other loose item.

Together they lugged the mattress. "This is what will save us," said Rock.

"Will it really destroy the entire complex?"

"I don't know. This is our insurance. I need you to get underneath all of this."

"Don't blow yourself up."

"No promises." He grabbed two rolls of toilet paper from under the sink.

Rock moved quickly through the house. He went back to the cupboard under the range and opened the valve as far as he could. Then he tied the ends of both rolls of toilet paper to the range. He rolled them all the way across the complex, taping them down on the floor. To the corridor with the stolen paintings. Back at the cupboard, he found a barbecue lighter and a tin of lighter fluid. Walking back to the room, he wet the toilet paper with accelerant. Hopefully it would function like a fuse.

The air was quickly becoming unbreathable. If Rock didn't leave, he'd be overcome. Already he felt nauseous. He waited until the last minute to shut the door to the corridor. Lighting a small bundle of toilet paper, he dropped it on the line of sheets rolled out on the floor. Fire ripped away, towards the kitchen.

Rock ran.

Out of the hallway. Shut the door to the bedroom. Past the box spring. Shut the washroom door. Shut off the lights. Lifted up the mattress and lay down next to Vivian, like Dracula entering his coffin for the night. It was dark and snug. She wrapped her arms around him, adjusting the mattress over his head

Nothing happened.

"I thought you lit the gas on fire."

"So did I."

"Well, when is this going to—"

The explosion whacked against them like they were hit by a baseball bat. The noise muffled by the mattress.

There was a giant thud. Followed by the sound of rocks and dirt collapsing.

Vivian screamed as the entire room tilted and began to slide.

57

The sliding motion stopped. Somehow the frame of the structure had shifted, then caught on something. Everything was in darkness. Rock switched on the flashlight wrapped to his wrist. "Are you okay?"

"Fine," said Vivian.

Rock sat up and pushed the mattress off. He stood up, and nearly fell forward. The floor was now sloping down. Carefully he walked towards the doorway. Vivian scrambled behind him, switching on her light.

Opening the door revealed nothing but blackness. Rock shone his flashlight beam on the floor, but found nothing. The bedroom had been swallowed by a giant hole. There was no sign of the bed, or the chamber below it.

Then the creaking started.

"The bathroom," said Vivian, "it's going to fall into that hole."

"Maybe," said Rock. He looked to his right. The remains of the bedroom floor was a ledge, jutting out over his head. He would have to lean over, then pull himself up.

"Can you make it?" asked Vivian.

"Sure. But will you?"

She punched him in the arm.

More creaking.

Rock jumped up, grabbing onto the exposed rebar. Slowly, his muscles in pain, he lifted himself up. Switching around, he pulled himself onto the ledge. He rolled around, onto his stomach. "Now, your turn."

Before Vivian could reach up, there was a thud. She scrambled backwards as the bathroom fell deeper into the sinkhole. What had been a two-foot leap had turned into six. And the creaking continued.

The floor below her began to slide down. She looked up to Rock. "I can't reach you."

He leaned out over the ledge, flailing his arms. "You'll have to jump."

"I can't. There's no way I'll make it. You go find something, a rug or a rope."

More creaking.

"There's no time," he said. "Jump."

Vivian backed up to the doorframe and took a running start. As she jumped the floor, and what was left of the bathroom, collapsed into the blackness. Her hand connected with Rock's arm. She was slipping. There was a huge crash as the bathroom landed in the darkness below.

Rock struggled with all his might to pull her up. Vivian curled her legs and swung upwards, grabbing Rock's shoulder with her right arm. He dragged her to safety.

"You're good," he said. "All that time in the climbing gym paid off for you."

"Never been climbing in my life," she said. They lay on the floor, catching their breath. After a few minutes they got up and headed out into the hallway with the stolen paintings. Every single one had been knocked off the wall.

Vivian shone her light down on a Cezanne. It was totally wrecked. "What a waste. Millions of dollars destroyed."

"My life is worth more than that," said Rock. The door to the main room had been blown off. Passing through the doorway, they saw small fires burning in the rubble. "The smoke isn't too bad for now. But we can't stay here for long..."

The two of them stopped, awestruck. Sunlight poked in from cracks in the kitchen wall. They ran toward the pile of rubble illuminated by the narrow shafts of light and began digging.

"Be careful," said Rock, "there could be knives or other mangled metal."

They cleared a path through the rubble, over the kitchen countertops. The room behind the range was even more of a wreck. The gas tank had exploded, plowing through the wall. A fireball must have burst forward, roasting everything in its path. Much of the complex was dark. Rock didn't want to wait around to inspect the damage.

They made their way to the outside wall. Rock took a large piece of concrete and began to hammer. The concrete had been poured over mesh metal, which was flimsier than Rock might have imagined. Once the weak concrete was chipped off, the mesh came away easier. It took the better part of an hour, but they scraped away a hole big enough to crawl through.

Together they pulled on a section of the metal mesh. With the two of them heaving, the fence separating the outside world came loose. They fell back against the rubble, but Rock bounced back up immediately, elated. He took Vivian's hand. They had an escape route.

"You go first," he said.

"Really?"

"Yeah."

Things are going to be okay, Rock thought.

She got her body halfway through, then stopped. She moved around, to examine the area around the hole. Then Vivian backed up, sat down. Put her head in her hands.

And began to cry.

"What?"

She couldn't speak, just waved to the hole.

Rock climbed out. His stomach sank.

Below, their only hope of exit was a two hundred foot drop off. A wall of smooth concrete on either side. Above, the surface topped out at the bottom of a rock overhang.

They were never getting out this way.

58

"What are we going to do?" said Vivian, wiping the tears from her cheeks.

"I need you to stay here. Keep watch. Try and signal somebody. With the tsunami coming, it's very likely people may walk by."

"But the canyon down there, it must be miles from the main road. There aren't any houses in sight."

"Stay here for now. I'm going to check the mineshaft. See if the route to the elevator is clear, okay? I'll be back in a couple of hours. Once I've figured out the state of the rest of the mine. You can look for water and something to make a rope with, but I'm not optimistic. And be careful of another gas leak."

"But you could suffocate."

"I'll head back the moment I feel light headed."

Rock moved to the stairwell that lead out of the complex. The door was dented from the explosion. The chamber beyond was dark, but undamaged. Maybe the fireball had cut the power to Dewey's bomb. They might have accidentally saved the day. Either way, Dewey wasn't coming back here. Not if he planned to blow the entire city up. He was probably on a flight to South America. Or Bermuda.

Rock entered the darkened shaft. His flashlight beam fell on a pile of rubble. Up ahead, the roof had collapsed. Should he dig through it? He decided it was the only option and began clearing it away with his bare hands.

It must have taken an hour to make progress. Rock was able to clear a break at the top of the pile, next to where the ceiling had caved in. He caught a glimpse of light. This made him even more eager to get to the other side. The rest of the mine still had power. Pushing his way through, he tumbled to the tracks.

Almost immediately came more shaking. More aftershocks. Rock felt rocks and dirt falling on his head. He got up and ran. Behind him a huge portion of the mineshaft collapsed. Plumes of dust billowed through the air. When it cleared, Rock felt a sinking feeling. How was he going to get back to Vivian?

Rock wondered if this was the right decision. Maybe he should have stayed in the complex. Tried to find another way out. He hadn't told Vivian about the tablet with the nuclear plans. If he had, she'd probably be down here with him. Risking her life. Rock had to make sure that the bomb got diffused. He was the only one who could do it. He'd had the training. Fate and coincidence had aligned to make that happen.

Rock's face was covered in soot as he trudged down the mineshaft. He wondered what had happened to the handcar. He wished he had it now. See if he could get it working. He and Vivian had made a mistake staying in Dewey's complex. The place was a tomb. They should have tried to escape from the beginning. If only their hormones hadn't got the better of them.

Rock arrived at the fork to the elevator. On the wall was a loose hose. He examined it. Water. Rock washed the dust off his face and continued on. He seemed to be making good time.

Until an earsplitting scream echoed down the shaft.

Rock stopped, listening for a collapse. When none came, he began to run towards the sound of the scream. Had Vivian gotten out, somehow? No one else should be down here.

He rounded a corner, and saw the end of the tunnel. It was dark, hard to see. Finally he caught sight of a figure in a chair, sitting in front of the elevator.

"Oh, my god, Vivian?"

She looked at Rock. Bound to the chair, she had a bandana covering her mouth.

Rock reached around to undo it. She went wild, screaming through the fabric.

"What is it?"

Vivian looked down. Rock saw the device strapped to her chest. Soft squares of packed brown material.

Connected with wires to an electronic device. With a timer counting down.

"Is this a bomb?"

Vivian nodded. She screamed wildly, muffled by the bandana. Rock didn't understand. Then he heard a click behind him. Something pressed against his head.

"She's trying to warn you about me."

Dewey stood right behind Rock, pointing a shotgun at his skull.

"Now, let's have a chat before you die."

59

"I'm so glad you found my manifesto," said Dewey. "The truth is, you two are the first to see it."

"Your edit could use a bit more finesse," said Rock.

"I don't see how." Dewey needled Rock with the shotgun.

"Are you planning to kill both of us?"

"I have no choice. This morning, out in the desert, I saw all the cars. All the people evacuating. There was no way my plan would work. What good is exploding a nuclear bomb, if no one's home? So I came back here to defuse it."

"Huh?" Rock looked at him in shock.

"That's right. But since I discovered you had blown my cover, and my bunker, I have no choice but to go through with my plans."

"You don't have to—"

"Spare me the speech. The plan's in motion. There's no way to stop me."

"You're going to blow the top off this mountain?"

Dewey laughed. "No, I'm going to blow up the crust of the earth under Los Angeles. Let it catch fire. I suppose you had time to examine the tools where I left you the last time."

"Yeah, but—"

"Next to that conveyor belt is a bore hole. Reaching down twenty-five kilometers into the earth. It's super hot. That's where the bomb will drop, hitting terminal velocity in a vacuum, once the air is sucked out of the hole."

"What is this?" said Rock. "Some kind of science experiment?"

"The computer simulation—"

"Bullshit. You have no idea what you're doing. That bomb won't destroy anything underground. The Soviets have been doing this for almost a century."

"Don't be so sure."

"Tell me, did you create the tsunami, too?"

Dewey smiled. "I doubt it. But who knows what causes earthquakes, right? This IS Los Angeles. Whole lotta shaking going on."

"And you think the army hasn't noticed you have one of their warheads."

"They've lost track of dozens. In China and Africa. One more won't make much of a difference. Besides, plenty of people in the government know who I am and what I intend to do. They've been surveilling me for months, but they have done nothing. The spies are hoping for an increase in their budgets. Most of those bureaucrats in Washington and Chicago can't stand California anyway. Tell them Los Angeles is going to fall into the ocean and they'd applaud."

"You'll be killing thousands of people."

"Millions have already died. In the Asian wars. But no one cares, because it's all happening in drips. What I'm doing is a bucket of ice water to the face." Dewey gazed at his feet. "If you knew the things I'd seen..."

Rock turned around. The gun barrel in his face. "That's what this is all about. You feel you're the victim in all this. So you have every right to fuck up other people's lives, because someone fucked you up."

"Exactly," said Dewey. "Time for me to play judge."

"Can I ask you a favor?"

"What?"

Rock looked down at the single-barreled shotgun. "Can you please lower that away from my face? If you're going to kill me, then shoot. Don't wave it around."

"Fine." Dewey produced a line of rope from a bag at his side. "Go over and stand next to Ms. Zhang."

Rock backed away. The rope in Dewey's hands snagged on something in the bag. His attention wavered only for an instant—

Rock leapt forward, knocking the shotgun up to the right. Then connected his boot with Dewey's left shin. Rock tried to grab hold of the weapon.

Dewey squeezed the trigger. The shot went wide, burying itself in the ceiling. Rock's ears roared with deafness and pain. The two men grappled with the gun, with Dewey doubled over in pain. Rock managed to get the weapon free. Then smacked the butt into Dewey's jaw.

Dewey fell down, crawling to the elevator, trying to take shelter behind Vivian.

Rock aimed the shotgun towards him.

For a moment the two men just stared at each other. Gradually Rock's sense of hearing came back.

"Don't shoot me," said Dewey, "I didn't mean to hurt you."

"I want the bomb disarmed."

Dewey smiled. "And what if I say no?"

Vivian screamed from the chair. She tried to move out of the way, to no avail.

"We don't have time for this," said Rock. Lowering the weapon in the direction of Dewey's leg, he pulled the trigger.

The action clicked into place. Nothing happened. The barrel was empty.

Dewey smiled and laughed. "You don't know much about guns, do you? That's a single shot."

Before Rock could move, Dewey produced an object from behind Vivian's chair. The pulse rifle, stolen from the Nicaraguans.

Rock saw a bright pink light, then felt himself falling. He dropped to his knees, then put his arms forward to cushion his face. Everything went numb, and blackness enveloped him.

Time passed in a void.

274

Gradually Rock awoke. He heard a far off screaming. It was Vivian. The bandana over her mouth had been removed. He stood up. "What's happening?" He stumbled towards her.

"The elevator," she said. "He went up to the parking garage."

Rock looked down at the bomb strapped to Vivian's waist. The counter had less than thirty seconds left. Rock reached over and tapped the elevator panel. The machinery hummed. He untied Vivian. Together they unstrapped the bomb.

The elevator doors opened. She walked inside. Rock pulled her back.

"What?"

He tossed the bomb in and hit the button for the parking garage before slipping out. The empty elevator went up its shaft.

Vivian took Rock's hand and they ran. As far away as possible. They got around a corner when everything shook. Fire roared up the tunnel. Rock dragged Vivian to the ground. When it was over he stood up and brushed himself off, then took her hand. "Are you okay?"

"Sure," she said. "But you know you've destroyed our only exit out of here."

"Don't be so sure," he said.

60

Rock looked down towards the elevator. The shaft was mostly collapsed. Black soot hung in the air. The lights went out.

"Just great," said Vivian, switching on her flashlight.

"Come on," said Rock, heading back. Vivian followed. "What happened?"

"I was in the house," she said. "He hit me with that cannon. Then I ended up at the elevator."

Rock passed her the tablet computer. "I found this when I was stopping the gas leak. It has all the plans to this complex." He loaded a set of blueprints. "There is an exit half a kilometer from here. This explains everything he wants to do. He wants to see Los Angeles burning for months."

"We've got to alert someone who can stop this."

"There's no time." Rock tapped the tablet, revealing a countdown. "Less that twenty minutes to go. I've got to stop it."

Vivian almost choked when she heard this. "How?"

"I've had training. By accident. On the last day of filming a movie."

"You're not a scientist."

"Its the only hope we've got."

"For a suicide mission? No, we've got to get out of here."

"You don't understand, it has to be stopped. Come this way."

Rock led them both to where the side tunnel met the main shaft. Just down the track they found the handcar. Got on and rode it down the tunnel another kilometer.

"Stop," said Rock. He hopped off. Examined the wall. Shined his flashlight into a narrow crevice. Rock wiped away years of soot to reveal boards. He heaved and kicked. The boards gave way. Revealing a shaft of light.

And a ladder. Leading up to the surface.

61

"I'm not leaving you."

"It doesn't matter," said Rock. "We're both pretty close to the end. There's no way you'll survive either, but at least you'll get a running start."

She shook her head.

"Go."

Reluctantly she moved to the ladder. As she started to climb, another aftershock hit. All around Rock the ceiling began to collapse. He jumped back to escape a pile of rubble. When the shaking stopped, the lights to the mineshaft came back on.

"Rock!" Her voice was coming from the top of the rubble.

"I can hear you."

"Are you—"

"I'm fine. Can you escape?"

"Yes."

"Are you injured?"

"No."

"Then go. I'm heading to the bomb. Good luck."

Vivian screamed for him to wait, but he kept going.

Rock discovered he was a lot closer to the conveyor belt than he thought. He reached the chamber just in time to see the large circular grate open, releasing a cloud of steam. He looked up at one of the monitors. Three minutes to go. The conveyor belt made a mighty rumble. The bomb slowly started to move towards the borehole.

Rock climbed up onto the conveyor belt, then onto the bomb. He remembered most weapons had an emergency shut down. A T-grip release—Rock found it and pulled. The handle ripped away.

Nothing happened.

This was fucked.

Dewey must have disabled it. Don't panic, you'll just have to dig a bit deeper. Rock moved in closer. With the back edge of his flashlight he quickly unscrewed the top control panel, revealing a mass of multicolored wires.

He fell into a technique he learned in acting classes. Sense memory. Trying to remember the feelings from some time earlier in your life. Rock thought it was stupid, but he was good at applying the same principle when he needed to remember technical details. He remembered von Stroheim's voice. The feel of the pliers.

This bomb was different. It had a red blinking light. That must indicate it was active. Distracting. Rock thought hard. He looked over to the borehole. The

280

conveyor belt dragged him closer. It was easily wide enough to swallow both Rock and the bomb together.

He looked down at the wires. A multicolored bundle, just like the mock up. Which one to cut? Was it the red one? And then the purple one, wasn't it? He snipped them both. The red light stayed on. As the countdown reached two minutes, thirty seconds, there was a massive rumbling. Oven-temperature heat blasted from the borehole. Straight from the center of the earth. Rock could barely stand it. It was getting too hot to hold the clippers.

He was going to pass out from the heat.

The green wire. It was the only chance.

Rock slipped off the conveyor belt.

Into the hole?

Then felt hands ripping him away. He fell to the ground, his fall broken by someone. He looked over.

Vivian.

"Why?"

"I didn't want to die alone."

She dragged him away from the scorching heat. Rock got up and ambled to the handcar.

Out of the corner of his eye he saw the bomb—the wires—and the red light.

Had he failed?

"We've got to go," said Vivian.

"No, but..."

"Unlock the brake."

As the countdown reached two minutes, the wires holding the bomb over the borehole released, sending it plunging down into the earth.

1980 "The Year The Past Disappeared"

The tablet in Rock's pocket sounded an alarm. "Two minutes to detonation. Clearing bore hole of air." A beeping. "Device in free fall," said the tablet, "terminal velocity in fifteen seconds."

Without a word, Rock began pumping the handcar, their only chance of escape.

62

Sweat dripped down Rock's chest, soaking his shirt. The wool of the navy sweater magnified the heat in the tunnel. What had he been thinking, choosing such a heavy garment? He pumped the handcar as fast as possible. They were really rolling down the track. Vivian helping out while keeping the brake in position.

In the distance Rock caught sight of rubble blocking their path. A cave-in next to their only route of escape. He stopped pumping and let the handcar coast.

"Slow down," he said, "get ready to stop."

Vivian leaned on the break, almost falling backwards. Rock reached forward and grabbed her, stopping a plummet to the ground.

"You okay?"

"I think so."

They came to a stop right before the collapsed ceiling.

"One minute, thirty seconds to detonation," chimed the tablet.

Rock hopped off, but Vivian was stuck. "The material in my jumpsuit," she screamed. "I can't get it free."

"This is not what we need right now." There are times in every person's life when something as simple as a piece of material caught in a brake lever can be a life or death situation. That is what panic can do to the human brain. A kind of tunnel vision, which had befallen Vivian. The effect was common after plane crashes. Many people will instinctively find a way out. But others will find simple tasks impossible, like undoing a lap belt, or extricating their feet from under the seat in front of them.

"Calm down," said Rock. He gripped the hand brake and pulled it toward him. "Now let go—"

"One minute, twenty seconds to detonation."

He pushed her forward as she got free of the brake. Vivian frantically climbed up the rubble pile, to a small space she'd burrowed between the rubble and the ceiling. She passed through with ease. But when Rock followed, his chest got stuck between the ceiling brace and the dirt. He pushed, but only made things worse.

"Come on," said Vivian. She rushed to him, digging away the rubble with her hands. Rock heaved back and forth. With a massive amount of force he flung himself forward, the brace collapsing behind him. But he was free.

"One minute, ten seconds to detonation."

Vivian stood up and guided him past the space he'd broken through earlier. They navigated the narrow passage to the ladder rungs bolted into the mountain. Daylight shone down from above.

Escape.

Vivian stopped to look up.

"Go," said Rock, pushing her forward. He looked up. And his heart sank. It was at least a hundred feet up. How could they climb that in a minute? He touched Vivian's arm. "Did you go to the top?"

"No."

"So we have no idea where this goes?"

She shook her head. "Better than staying down here."

They started to climb.

And they moved fast. The shaft narrowed considerably after the first ten feet. Halfway up, Rock began to feel claustrophobic. Even if he fell, he probably wouldn't make it to the bottom. Unless his body plunged completely vertically, like an Olympic diver.

Twenty feet from the top, one of the ladder rungs under Vivian's foot gave way. Rock heard the clanging and ducked out of the path of the rusty piece of metal at the last moment. Vivian lost her balance and started falling. Rock caught her and held on.

"Thanks," she said.

"Forty seconds to detonation," chimed the tablet.

Vivian climbed faster, pulling away from Rock.

With ten feet to go, Rock felt himself out of breath, exhausted. He wasn't a young man, despite all the hours in the gym, and the salads he'd eaten.

"Twenty seconds to detonation."

He watched as Vivian's figure blocked the light. She emerged onto the surface, then disappeared. She wasn't screaming. Maybe they'd found a safe spot to wait this out.

285

Rock collected all his energy and began climbing. His mind drifted to the blast. Would it completely destroy the mountain? Making this escape hopeless? He thought of those old Soviet movies where entire craters were created from detonating bombs underground. They both might be dead in thirty seconds anyway.

Rock looked up. Saw the beautiful blue sky. At the western edge, a wall of dark clouds approached. Ominous. Foreshadowing? All these thoughts passed through his brain in a split second.

The tablet began to count down from ten.

Rock emerged at the top. He looked to his right. Vivian screamed in panic.

"What?"

Rock saw the shadow first, towering over him. He turned around.

Dewey.

With his shotgun.

He hit Rock in the jaw with the butt.

Rock fell backwards into the shaft, darkness enveloping everything. He didn't even feel the bomb explode.

63

Ira knew he was insane. If he survived this, his wife would surely leave him. But this boat was more important to him than anything else. It wasn't just the money. He refused to let a tsunami destroy it before he could take it on a sea voyage. His wife, children and extended family were all safe. He had lied to them, saying he was outside Bakersfield, when in actual fact he had heard the tsunami warning and immediately driven to Marina del Rey, to get the yacht out of the harbor before the giant wave made landfall.

It was also a once-in-a-lifetime opportunity to experience an enormous wave. Call it a stunt. Or a death wish. He wasn't going to have his new boat wrecked upon the shores of Southern California without his body in it.

Pulling up to the dock, Ira was surprised that he wasn't the only one. Others, all men, were also unmooring their boats in a dreaded determination to protect their investments. This yacht club might be on its way to becoming a mass gravesite.

Ira kept the sails stowed, using the diesel motor to putter out of the marina, away from the boats coming in from Santa Catalina island. The last thing he needed to do was get in the way of people evacuating.

In the main cabin he watched a satellite feed of the area on his monitor. The high-resolution orbital observatory had trained its cameras on the southland. In realtime he watched the wave approach. It didn't look like a tidal wave, but it was there. Ready to kill. There were also dozens of helicopters and planes watching from the air, with the worst damage predicted to hit the airport.

Ira looked back. The shore was far behind him, little more than a thin grey line on the horizon. Then he looked ahead.

A wall.

A wall of dark grey water. Facing the boat at a ninety-degree angle.

The craft titled back, flinging Ira to the deck. He skidded to the back wall of the cabin, barely missing the open door. If he had been flung through the doorway, he wouldn't have a chance. The boat crested the wave, leveling out.

Then the boat fell, like a cart on a roller coaster, over the other side of the mountain of water. Ira held on, terrified. Helpless. It felt like the boat would fall end over end, capsizing. Fear tensed his body, looking death right in the eye.

Then the bang.

Like a giant clap of thunder.

It came from behind the boat.

Ira looked behind, peering out the doorway, but saw nothing. Only blue-grey water. As the boat leveled off, his eyes drifted back to the monitor, the image zoomed in on Los Angeles. He saw something he never imagined.

Shock waves.

Rushing over the city. As if the houses and roads and trees rode a tidal wave underneath the ground. Not one, but several, emanating from the Hollywood Hills. The waves were there, but they weren't, at the same time. You could see the land transform, then settle back. The earth rippled, like a carpet unfurling.

The ripples reached the sea. Transforming into giant tidal waves erupting from the beach.

Heading right for the tsunami.

And Ira's boat.

The two giant waves crashed into each other. The ocean wave was no match for that from the beach. Ira looked back and shut the door to the cabin.

Twice in a matter of minutes. Like a cork in a bathtub.

The giant wave rolled under the boat flinging it back. The hull and the masts groaned under the pressure, but, miraculously, did not splinter apart.

If Ira had looked up he would have seen a helicopter. It was usually there to relate traffic reports for KXXX. But today Doug sat in the passenger seat, describing the wave they were chasing out over the ocean.

289

1980 "The Year The Past Disappeared"

"I've never seen anything like this before," said Doug, babbling into his headset microphone. "It's like a battle between two tectonic plates playing out in the sea. The shock wave snapped through the city, but hasn't seemed to do much damage. We haven't seen major fires or building collapses. It's as if all the kinetic energy was offloaded into the water. Counteracting the tsunami arriving from the far ocean."

The helicopter hit a mass of fog and dark clouds. He shivered as freezing cold air rushed into the cockpit.

64

It was the scald of hot steam that made Rock regain consciousness. A huge torrent was flooding the shaft, water vapor rising as the boiling liquid climbed ever higher. Rock had landed on his tailbone, stuck between ladder rungs and a horizontal support. The bomb had set off some kind of underwater spring. The escape shaft was turning into a geyser.

Rock pushed himself off the wall and scrambled up the rungs. As he got to the opening at the top, his feet felt the scald of the water. He reached the surface and pushed off, rolling out of the way as the water shot upwards. He ran up the side of a nearby slope as the boiling water shot skyward—as it landed, turning the barren hillside to mud.

His view was partially obscured by the geyser. Through the shower he saw Dewey dragging Vivian towards his pickup. Her hands and ankles were tied up with bright yellow rope as he tossed her in the passenger side of the truck's cab. Rock couldn't believe a wreck like that was still on the road. It had to be at least forty years old. One thing Rock remembered about the desert was that it kept ancient vehicles perfectly preserved.

"Stop," she yelled.

"No way," said Dewey, "you're my little bargaining chip if I can't get across the border."

Rock knew if Dewey escaped with her, she'd certainly be killed. He broke out of his daze, dodging the scalding fountain, chasing after the truck. But it was too late. Dewey tore away from the geyser as fast as the vehicle could go, kicking up a giant cloud of dirt.

Rock stopped, watching the truck disappear down a hill. Beside him, in the gap in the trees, he saw a view that stretched out over the city. So much for the tsunami.

As he moved closer to the woods, he caught sight of the road again. It curved sharply, almost in a loop. Which meant Dewey couldn't gun it all the way down the mountain. Not without doubling back. Maybe Rock could cut him off. How fast could the truck go on a dirt road? Especially with ancient brakes and handling?

Rock clambered down the mountain as fast as he could. He avoided trees and shrubs. He leapt off a rocky outcrop, landing in bushes ten feet below. He was almost there.

As he moved out of the trees he saw the road was cut into the mountain, leaving an embankment of about ten feet above the gravel. Barely wide enough to accommodate two vehicles. Two narrow modern vehicles, not a truck from the 1980's. But if Dewey passed by slow enough, he could jump on. He headed along the overhang, looking for a spot obscured from a vehicle coming down the mountain.

A minute passed. Rock grew restless. No sign of the truck. And no growl of an ancient combustion engine. You could hear one of those a mile away. If the car had been electric there was no way Rock would get away with this plan. Of course, Dewey might have turned off another road that Rock didn't know about. Or maybe Rock had been too late.

And what was he going to do? Dewey had a shotgun. Rock had... his Swiss army flashlight. With a knife to cut through Vivian's bindings. That was it, besides his boots and knuckles. It would have to do. She would die if he didn't act. Dewey wouldn't leave any witnesses if he could avoid it.

Rock was snapped out of his thoughts by a rumble coming down the mountain.

65

Rock flew through the air. The truck was moving faster than he expected. He missed the bed, his arms slamming into the rear tailgate. Frantically his hand latched on, his feet felt the dirt road below. Small stones nicked off the truck's exterior, pelting his legs, a few walloping off his skull.

Dewey saw all this from the rear-view mirror. "What the hell's he doing? Screw him." He swerved the steering wheel wildly back and forth.

"No," said Vivian.

The engine screamed as Dewey hit the gas. The dash began to rattle violently. The truck didn't like this speed. With tortuous groans the vehicle hit eighty miles an hour. Vivian leaned over to Dewey and did the first thing that came into her head.

She bit. Deeply.

The teeth grabbed something. She dug in deep like a vampire. Then pulled back and spat out. Possibly a flap of skin. Vivian looked over. She had hit one of his arteries. Blood spurted from the wound. Dewey screamed. He took a hand off the wheel to stop the bleeding. Surprisingly, with Dewey's attention split, the truck straightened out. Even as it continued to plow down the mountain road.

Dewey took his leg off the gas pedal. Elbowed Vivian away with as much force as he could muster, while pressing against the wound. "What did you do, you crazy bitch?"

Blood flew everywhere. The windshield, the radio, the rear-view mirror. Everything sprayed in red. Dewey buttoned his collar to stem the bleeding.

Vivian attacked again, biting him on the ear. Trying to rip off his earlobe.

In the back, Rock got a foothold on the rear bumper. Pushed himself over onto the flatbed. Took a moment to catch his breath. He was an old fogey. Acting like a teenage stuntman. As the truck straightened out, Rock realized this was his opportunity. He lunged toward the cab of the truck, lowering himself down to the running boards.

He tried the door. It was locked. Rock climbed in the passenger side window as Vivian viciously attacked Dewey again. He looked up, appalled by the gristly scene in front of him. He was comforted only slightly when he saw it was Dewey, not Vivian, who had their blood splashed everywhere. As he dragged himself through the window, he pushed Vivian towards Dewey. Flicking open the knife from the base of the flashlight, he cut away the ropes binding her ankles. She stared back at him, her face blood-streaked. Nodding, she leaned her wrists out towards Rock to cut free.

The narrow cliff side embankment flattened out. Dewey turned the truck to the right. Off the road. Down a hill that was less sheer than before, although littered with trees and shrubs. Still, the truck got through. Near the bottom the road appeared again. The truck flew up a lipped knoll, blocking the drainage ditch. Then flew through the air. There was a huge thunk as they plowed through a bush. And kept going.

Vivian's hands were free. She attacked Dewey even harder. Rock leaned over, trying to grab him by the collar. Vivian straddled a leg between Dewey's and stomped down on the brake. The engine groaned and ground to a halt.

Dewey didn't care. He tore at his shirt. Ripping a strip of cloth to tie around his neck. The only way he'd stop the bleeding. With him distracted, Rock opened the passenger door, pulling Vivian out, tossing her on the ground.

Rock got back in and aimed his pocketknife at Dewey, who hit the accelerator. The truck lurched forward. One hand on the wheel, the other defending against the knife blade, which, to be truthful, wasn't difficult.

"I'm ready to go straight to hell," said Rock, grabbing the wheel.

1980 "The Year The Past Disappeared"

"You're insane," said Dewey.

Rock burst out laughing. There was no other way to respond.

Dewey let go of the steering wheel, grabbing a shotgun with his left arm. Aimed it right at Rock, who scrambled out the passenger door window. Dewey propped the gun against his armrest and fired. Rock dragged himself onto the hood as the shotgun blast flew past his leg. He gripped onto the lip of the hood by the windshield.

Dewey laughed. He had him now.

The truck flew up over a second embankment. Onto another stretch of narrow dirt mountain road. This one with a guardrail. Protecting traffic from a sheer drop off.

Rock looked over his shoulder.

Less than thirty feet ahead, the entire road was washed out by a landslide.

66

Rock had expected the truck to land in the washout with a thud, in a wreck of metal or an explosion. But instead it just slid down the walls of the gully. Rock barely held on as Dewey kept on going, a man gone mad. He was looking for a way to kick Dewey out of the front seat. If Dewey wanted to use the shotgun again, he'd have to reload.

The car slowed down. The passenger door flew wide open. Rock knew he had to get off the hood. With exhausted muscles he pulled himself around to the passenger side door. Pushed himself back into the cab. Dewey was fumbling with a box of shotgun shells. The car heaved again, parallel to the road. The driver's side door faced the cliff. The box of shells fell from Dewey's hands, sprinkling all over the floor below the steering wheel.

Rock grabbed the barrel of the gun. Dewey pulled back, shooting Rock a look of evil. As he struggled to get the gun out of Dewey's hands, Rock caught a glimpse through the front window.

"Stop, hit the brake—"

"What?" said Dewey, totally focused on the weapon.

"The road—"

Around the truck went. Sliding with mud and other debris to the edge of the cliff. When the vehicle came to a stop, Dewey opened his door, not taking his hands off the weapon. He looked down.

The truck was about to go over.

Dewey stepped out, he'd be going for a long fall before he hit solid ground.

The only way out was past Rock. Rather than negotiate, Dewey decided to fight. He lurched forward, thrusting the gun into Rock's shoulder.

Then an aftershock hit. The ground holding up the rear driver's side wheel collapsed. The car jolted, flinging Dewey out.

His feet dangled over open air.

With one arm he gripped the plastic handle on the door, which opened wide, dangling him over the precipice.

Rock rushed over. "Give me your hand, I'll pull you to safety."

Dewey latched on to him. Swung over to the cabin, clawing at Rock's face.

Rock tried to shake him off. "What the hell are you doing?"

"You're one of them."

"Huh?"

"The establishment. The people. In this town. In Hollywood. You don't know what they did to my father. And my sister."

"Let go of me," said Rock, trying to pry him off, while simultaneously bracing them both so they wouldn't fall out.

"You're never going to stop it," said Dewey.

"This whole thing is going to fall off the cliff. Give me your hand. I'll pull you clear."

Dewey took Rock's hand and dragged him forward. He got a foothold against the running boards...

...but used it...

...to pull Rock out of the truck...

Rock flailed furiously, catching sight of the ground a hundred feet below. He didn't want to die. His muscles screamed in pain as he wrapped his arm around the steering column.

"What the hell are you doing?"

Dewey grinned. "You're coming with me. We're going to the pits of Hades. Together."

Rock kicked Dewey in the chest. The guy winced in pain, but wouldn't let go. Rock kicked again, this time to the throat. The crunch of bone whipped through the air. Still Dewey kept a steel grip on Rock. A gurgle erupted from Dewey's throat. To Rock it sounded like laughter. He pulled Rock further out of the truck.

Enough was enough. It was time to kill.

Rock kicked, again and again. Dewey's head turned red with welts and blood. With one last heave, Rock's boot hit a massive blow to the center of his face. The grip loosened. Dewey fell away. Screaming.

Rock looked down as the miniscule figure walloped off a boulder, bouncing around like a rag doll before coming to a still pause at the bottom of the gully.

Rock took a deep breath. It was all he had time to do before the shaking started again.

67

The truck slid sideways. Rock held on, clinging to the steering wheel as the ground below the vehicle collapsed. He grabbed desperately at the seat as the vehicle angled down sideways. Then it stopped. But it was teetering on the edge. The front left wheel jutted out over empty space. Dewey had almost dragged him out of the truck. Rock's legs dangled as he used all his upper body strength to pull himself back in the cab. It might not be enough to save him.

He winced in pain as he pushed himself up onto the bench seat. The truck was on a slope that was giving way. Loose bits of gravel knocked off the body of the truck, sounding a hollow echo. The whole thing was about to teeter off the edge before he could escape out the passenger side.

Rock caught a glimpse in the rear-view mirror. Vivian emerged from the woods. Running towards the truck. She saw what was happening and put all her weight down on the rear tailgate.

Rock scrambled across the seat and dove out the passenger door as the truck tumbled top over end. Vivian joined him, as the vehicle plummeted to the ground. Smashing with a boom. But no explosion. It was upside down, the gas tank still intact.

"How anti-climactic," said Rock. "I was expecting a real fireworks show."

Vivian hugged him. He met her lips with a welcoming kiss. She nuzzled her forehead against his. "After seeing you alive, I'll never wish for anything else again."

"Thank you," he said, "for saving my life."

Vivian smiled. "Now we're even."

He took her hand and they walked back up to the road. When they got there, Rock began to shiver. "What's up with this weather? It's so cold."

"That bomb did something weird to the atmospheric pressure," said Vivian. "Look at the sky."

"So you're the meteorologist now?"

"Look."

Rock turned around. The landslide had cut a hole in the trees, leaving a spectacular view of the city, all the way to the ocean. Over the water dark clouds painted the horizon.

It was Vivian's turn to shiver. Rock reached over and zipped up her jumpsuit. "You've got to learn about how to live in a cold climate."

"I go to Big Bear every year." She looked around. "The air. It's heading below the freezing mark. That isn't normal."

A great thunderclap erupted from the sky. Then more lightening. But instead of rain, a heavy flurry began to fall.

"Snow," said Vivian. "In Los Angeles."

They stood there, watching the city consumed by a blizzard.

"Did you bring your skis?" asked Rock.

68

"I've never seen this side of L. A.," said Rock. "All this greenery and woods. For the last fifteen years I've only come into town for meetings. And when we're shooting. Usually I head to the studio straight from the airport. I never had time to go hikeing."

The dirt road meandered through the hills. It had continued to snow, at times growing heavy. They had navigated two other rockslides. But had yet to see any major damage, despite the bomb. Dewcy's plan to light the entire city on fire hadn't happened. It was sad, thought Rock. Even in death, he'd been upstaged by natural events.

Taking a shortcut through the woods, they even saw a deer. Sipping water from the Hollywood reservoir.

The closer they got to civilization, the more physical distance Rock and Vivian put between each other. "I'd really like to phone my wife," said Rock. "She'll be worried about me."

"Yeah," said Vivian, "I need to talk to my husband."

Just past the reservoir, they reached the 101 freeway. Walking underneath it, Rock was shocked by the destruction. Everywhere lay the smoldering wreckage of cars. Ascending a hill on the other side, Rock looked back in awe. "My god, can you believe this happened?"

The wrecks had been moved to the side of the highway, like a black strip added to the roadway. In some places little more than a lane's width remained.

They continued on, passing the Hollywood Bowl. The vast parking lot had been turned into a junkyard. Despite the state of the freeway, it was almost full with ruined vehicles.

Vivian shook her head. "This is going to take months to clean up."

They found another hiking trail, leading up to Mulholland Drive. Every single house they passed had some evidence of fire damage. A couple dwellings had completely burnt down. Rock shook his head. "People must have been lucky to get out with their lives."

They reached a look off and stopped. The city was dotted with smoldering fires. In the far distance, somewhere downtown, an office tower burned, sending a stream of black smoke into the clouds.

"I want to go back to the park," said Vivian.

"What's that...?"

"To the dog park. See if I could find my phone."

Rock examined her miserable expression. She knew her dog was dead. "It's been three days."

"I want to check anyway."

308

As they started up again, a group of two guys and two girls approached, heading to the look off. Rock was shocked when he saw one of them was Dougie.

"How're you doing?" said Rock. "What are you up to?"

Dougie's eyes widened. "Mr. MacLean. I can't believe you're here."

One of the girls eyed Vivian. "Aren't you the traffic reporter—"

"Yeah."

"What are you guys doing here?" said Dougie.

"It's a long story," said Rock. "It'll all come out in the papers soon enough."

Dougie shook his head. "I don't know, man. I'm not sure I'm cut out for L.A. life. This is just too far out for me. It might be time to head back to Iowa. Or maybe I can get some film job in Chicago, or something."

"This is an anomaly," said Vivian. "It's not always quite this bad."

"Not always," said Rock. "Just sometimes."

Dougie looked at their costumes. "Why are you dressed in uniforms? Did your house in Santa Monica get hit by the tsunami?"

"No one got hit," said the girl, contradicting him. "It was cancelled."

It was at this point that Rock realized that Dewey and his friends were really, really high. "You guys didn't evacuate?"

"Well," said Dougie, "we're staying in the hills, house sitting. We're kind of getting paid to be here."

The other guy in the group lit up a joint. Passed it around. Even Vivian took part in the session, despite the fact she hadn't gotten high in twelve years. It made Rock happy. Something familiar.

"You can come to our place," said Dougie. "We've got lots of food, weed, and bottled water. And a barbecue."

"It's okay," said Rock. "We've got to go find Vivian's dog. And I have to walk all the way back to Santa Monica."

"The power's out, so be careful."

One of the girls played with her phone. "We've got internet back." The tsunami warning's been cancelled, see—" she turned the screen around for everyone to look. "There was a second tsunami that destroyed the first. It's like, a phenomenon."

"Is that why it's snowing?" said Vivian.

The wind began to pick up. "We'd better get going," said Rock, shivering. "Take care. Make sure you wear lots of warm clothing."

Rock and Vivian headed off, down the Mulholland trail, until they came to a residential street. There wasn't a soul in sight as they wandered down through the hills.

"Wow," said Vivian. "We really do have the whole city to ourselves."

As the sky cleared, leaving a layer of snow on the ground, they reached Runyon Canyon Park. They searched for an hour, but it wasn't until they found a public fountain that Vivian heard Finnegan's familiar bark. He was tied up, but the fountain had provided him something to drink, keeping him alive through the crisis. Vivian cuddled the dog like a lost child.

Rock was less overwhelmed with sentimentality. He looked to the west. They were standing at just the right angle to catch a glimpse of the Hollywood sign in the distance. The 'ood' letters at the end had completely collapsed in a landslide.

Vivian saw it, too. "Look at that."

"They'll fix it," said Rock, "or maybe they'll finally tear it down. Unless this is what passes for culture out here."

"I guess."

They began a long trudge back to the North Fuller gate. Passing through the dog park area, something caught Vivian's eye. She walked through the gate to the off leash area. Her phone was still there, slightly wet from the melting snow.

Rock watched as she talked to her husband. For the first time in many years, he felt a sense of regret.

69

Rock heard the sound of the helicopter first. "Is that...?"

"Yeah. The KXXX news chopper. My husband's in it right now. Got it to divert." The helicopter landed on a clear patch of grass about fifty feet away. Vivian stopped when she saw Rock wasn't moving towards it. "Come on. Get in. They'll take you to Santa Monica."

Vivian scooped up Finnegan in her arms. "You could be injured. Or something. I'm not taking any risks. We should go to a hospital."

"If I die on the walk home, tell my wife I love her."

Vivian scowled at him.

"Or contact my agent."

Vivian waved goodbye, and, without another word, headed to the open door of the helicopter. This chapter of her life, it seemed, was over. She got in and Doug hugged and kissed her. Then helped buckle her safety belt.

Doug looked out the window. "Is that Rock MacLean?"

"Yup."

"Does he need a lift?"

"Nope. He'll walk."

"Jesus," said Doug. "What if he gets attacked by looters?"

"He's a tough guy. He'll make it."

Doug took Finnegan. "Did you miss me?"

"More than ever."

Doug sniffed the air. "Have you been smoking something?"

Rock waved as the chopper took off. Then he left the park, continuing down the hill to Santa Monica Boulevard. He followed it all the way to the beach. The whole walk, not a car in sight.

As Rock got towards Third Street, he stopped at a liquor store that had been abandoned. He looked inside. The power was still on. The person running it had just taken up and left, leaving it unlocked. Probably presumed the tsunami would get it.

He grabbed a backpack for sale on the shelves. Filled it with beer, vodka, and lime cordial. Cigarettes. Also grabbed some frozen hamburgers, cheese and buns. It wasn't much, but it would sustain him until things got back to normal. He wrote down the name of the store and the prices of things he had taken. At his salary, it looked petty to be stealing. He'd come back later and pay in cash.

Rock lugged his stash back to the house on Third Street, which was undamaged. Actually, he was surprised by the lack of destruction in most of the city, except for the cars. He found a cell phone, but the battery was dead. While it charged, he started the barbecue. He would call his wife, then the airport. One last night alone until he faced the music.

When the phone was charged, he barely had time to get a hold of Candy, and tell her he was all right. Then the cell service cut out. He sent her a text saying he would call again tomorrow. Then went back to the barbecue. Just as the burgers were almost ready, Rock heard sobbing from next door.

A car had driven up just before sundown. Rock wandered out to Tasha's back garden. He found a bearded man in khakis and a dress shirt. Thick glasses. "Are you okay?"

The man wiped his eyes. "No. My wife lived here."

The statement hit Rock like a brick wall. "What happened?"

The man looked up. "You're an actor."

"Yeah. I live next door. Can I offer you a drink?"

"Sure." The man stayed silent until he got to Rock's backyard and downed half a beer. "Did you know her?"

For a moment Rock considered confessing his relationship. That was what people do at wakes, wasn't it? Tell happy stories about the dead. But this man didn't need another layer of grief.

"No," said Rock. "I never know my neighbors."

70

The Air Canada Boeing 888 touched down at Island Airport, the gleam of Lake Ontario reflecting off the silver surface of the bank towers that dotted the shore. With an underground tunnel that took you right into downtown in minutes, Toronto Island had become the busiest airport in North America, second only to Los Angeles. The only problem was the water. It created treacherous crosswinds and frequent bouts of localized precipitation. Which meant landings were often rough. Rock always feared the plane would fall off into the lake. Make the passengers swim for their lives.

Rock had gone through customs in Los Angeles, so he had an hour and a half to wait before his flight to Cape Breton. Being back in Canada felt so artificial. It was so damn safe here. No crime, no danger, no excitement. Especially in Toronto. It might have been the country's second largest city, but it was number one for personal safety.

1980 "The Year The Past Disappeared"

Rock sat in the Terminal 3 Tim Horton's, watching the live news stream on a giant screen across from the sitting area. The latest polls said the California and Oregon referendums might pass, but the Quebec referendum was doomed. He felt bad, almost, for the Quebec separatists. They deserved respect, but they never got it from the power brokers in English Canada. In their own way, they were like Dewey. This was the forth time they'd gone to the people. It must be awful to see your dreams crushed so many times. How could you still believe? Yet they still kept trying.

It was times like this, waiting in an airport, that he wished he had a private plane. Earlier in his career he had considered buying one and paying a crew. But then he'd worked on a docudrama about a plane crash in Eastern Transvaal in the 'eighties. It had made his skin crawl. He discovered how political those accident inquests are. That's why they never do them for private air services. You fly at your own risk. With commercial airlines there are major national interests at stake when it comes to safety. But with a private jet it's...well... private. Governments don't have the time or money to care.

He sipped his coffee. It tasted good. Hell, there was so much cream and sugar in the cup, he could have been drinking gasoline and he wouldn't have noticed.

He made sure he called Candy to tell her the arrival time. She was worried that Ira was missing. He was the first person she'd gotten a hold of when this whole mess started. Even Rock couldn't believe he'd gone off in his boat.

An hour later he filed into the turboprop airplane. Spent the next two hours to Sydney reading a script by Randy Campbell. For a movie he thought was crap, little more than a shaggy dog story. But it might pay well.

Sydney had one of only two commercial airports in Nova Scotia. It was quaint, like a child's toy. Two gates—arrivals and departures. Its simplicity made Rock smile every time he walked off the plane. A far cry from the zoo of LAX.

Yet, tonight, there were photographers waiting for him as he entered the terminal.

Rock was barraged with questions as he searched for his wife. He made a brief statement, expressing his regret for what happened in L.A., then directed the journos to contact his publicist.

Through the crowd he caught sight of Candy.

"Daddy! Daddy!"

His two little girls ran up. He hugged them. Looked up at their mother. Rock gazed into his wife's eyes, silently. Then she took his hand. And they walked to the car as a family.

71

Two months later, Rock was back in a trailer on the Universal lot. He had to be in Los Angeles for a week. The Man In the High Castle needed reshoots. The studio had changed the name of the film to 'Rampage!' after the longer original title fared poorly with focus groups. They were trying to play down the science fiction element.

Rock was back in his Nazi uniform. It was beginning to feel like an old pair of underwear. Uncomfortable at first, now almost used to it.

The summer was in full swing. Rock had spent the last few weeks in Cape Breton. With Candy and the kids at their summer house on the Bras d'Or Lakes. Almost every day they went swimming. Most nights were barbecues. Candy and Rock had never talked about his indiscretions, aided by the fact that the news media had more important things to report. No one had investigated Rock or Vivian's role in Dewey's plan, and neither of them had volunteered the information.

Plenty of people had come to visit the house. Making sure he was okay. Even Ira, the lost sailor, had made it back to shore, only to declare a two-month holiday for him and his wife. They had sailed down through the Panama Canal, and up to Nova Scotia. It had taken longer than he expected, so Rock had helped him find a berth in Ben Eion. He would sail it back next summer. As a gesture of gratitude, Ira had given Rock use of the boat for the rest of the summer.

So amidst this laid-back existence, Rock wasn't pleased to have the reshoot clause in his contract activated. Whenever a movie is made, each day after the scenes are shot the editor makes an assembly. A very rough edit of the scene, without music. That way, the production team can see any obvious problems they may have missed during filming. Like shots that don't match, or a terrible performance, or bad sound. To discover any major disasters before the end of principle photography. However, these daily assemblies give no clue to how the movie is playing over a full two hours. Audiences might not understand certain plot points, or an emotional moment might not play right. The financier, or in this case the studio, has a contingency budget to cover this. Usually five days to re-shoot, sometimes less. Almost never more, except in the case of severe problems.

Most of the past two days he'd spent doing nothing. Except gloating at the fact that Simpson, as expected, had been fired. It was no surprise that the ex-director had announced his engagement to Samantha. Rock hoped the two of them were happy.

Cochese had taken over the center seat. Which was a big deal for him. He was the only Native American working in the Director's Guild. Rock was feeling a lot better about the film. Much of the reshoots were minor things. People who had seen the rough cut told him the film played much better than anyone expected. Even if no one went to see it in theaters, the film would have a life.

Everything was going well, until Randy Campbell came in after lunch. "Look," said the balding director from Prince Edward Island, "we're going to use a groundbreaking photo projection animation technique that's never been done before. We're not making a movie, we're making history."

Rock winced. "I'm just not sure that I want to be an actor anymore."

"We've got the money to pay you well. And all you've got to do is sit in a recording studio for a week. You can do it in your pajamas."

"But I promised my wife."

"Voice work doesn't count."

"I just don't feel like coming back here after what I've been through."

Randy smiled. "Hey buddy, I understand. If I had it my way, I'd relocate all the studio front offices to Santa Barbara, or New Zealand, or Vancouver."

"I feel like I'm in a crisis," said Rock. "What am I going to do for the rest of my life?"

Randy shook his head. "The roller coaster ride has to end sometime. You didn't expect this career to last forever?"

"No."

"So be glad you got off while you can still learn new tricks. That's better off than those poor schmucks who become celebrity poker players."

72

Rock was shopping at the Ralphs in west Los Angeles. It made him happy. Ever since he was a child he had enjoyed perusing the aisles of grocery stores. And this store, on Olympic, was dominated by a giant parking lot in the front. The soullessness and sense of suburbia it offered was complete and reassuring. You never had to worry about the clerk saying hi to you or knowing your dietary habits, because the people working there didn't care. That's the way Rock liked it.

He drove himself there. The streets were so clear. The city was still clearing up all the wrecks. Insurance rates had skyrocketed, so many people were holding off buying a new vehicle for as long as possible. Many had given up on the automobile. New habits were being formed out of the ashes of the old Los Angeles.

1980 "The Year The Past Disappeared"

A million people had left the city, or had died in the calamity. Many more swore they'd never get into a car again.

Still, it made the drive along Santa Monica much more pleasant.

Rock wandered the aisles of the supermarket, crowded with people getting off work. Perusing the different types of Thai chilies, he was distracted by a woman examining the sweet potatoes. It was Vivian. Something was different. Her body was bigger. Then Rock figured it out.

She was pregnant.

"Did you know those aren't actually yams?" said Rock, walking up.

"I know. I've been to Jamaica." She looked at him with an unwavering glance. Pride, happiness, and a cool distance, all rolled into one.

Rock looked down at her stomach. "When's your due date?"

"Next January." She leaned into his ear. "Don't worry, it's not yours."

"Guaranteed?"

Vivian's face glowed at him, but her lips remained silent. She moved past him, brushing his hand. She didn't say goodbye.

Rock went back to the chilies. Picked out some that looked ripe. And headed to the checkout. No one stared. For a moment he thought about Vivian's child. Then put it out of his mind and got in line.

**Don't miss the next chapter in
The Tsunami Trilogy**

The
Two
Day
March

**Turn the page for a preview of
The Two Day March...**

Part One
The Last Monday in April

1

The guy was twitching. He'd boarded about thirty minutes before. At some out-of-the-way station at the edge of an out-of-the-way farming community. After a brief glance at the other passengers in the car, he headed straight for Dewey.

The only white person in sight.

There were plenty other vacant seats on the train. The compartment was far from even a quarter full. Certainly nothing like Dewey had grown accustomed to in Tokyo. But it was a given that the guy was going to ask to practice his (probably terrible) English. Or he would open a textbook, and casually approach Dewey with a question about grammar. It had happened before. And always on a rural train line. It would happen, of course, in the most awkward manner possible.

One of Dewey's Danish coworkers, despite the fact he spoke English in a manner indistinguishable from a North American, became monolingual on such occasions. It was just reality that all Japanese people assumed every white person was an American.

But this guy was worse. He twitched.

At first it was just the nervous left leg, bobbing up and down. Then both legs started. A perfunctory game of inter-view-the-foreigner couldn't be far off now.

When Dewey had first come to Japan, his company had given him training on Japanese etiquette. Restless legs were a definite no-no. Especially around a stranger. So Dewey could only conclude that the guy next to him was either mentally ill or really didn't like him. It was a way of making a statement without saying anything.

Dewey Lane was only thirty-one years old, but he had sat next to all different kinds of Japanese people. Who had exhibited all kinds of strange behaviors in the presence of a foreign person. Actually, it wasn't that he was a foreigner, but that he was... visibly foreign. Clearly A WHITE PERSON. Most Japanese people only got nervous around other Asian people once they heard them speak. The air violated with the tones of Chinese, Korean, or some other language from further south along the Pacific Rim. Or Mongolia.

One night Dewey had been heading back on the Hibiya line from the Ginza area of Tokyo. The only place to stand was in front of a fat, dweeby-looking guy. Who spent the entire trip picking his nose and eating it. Then there were the numerous number of those who simply got up and walked away the moment a white person sat next to them. Or the people, usually on the Saikyo Line, and other trains heading north out of Tokyo, who felt the need to turn on their cell phone's television application and watch it, at high volume, without headphones.

A few years earlier, the Japanese companies who made mobile phones—which only functioned with the Japanese cell network—had developed the TV feature. To watch over-the-air broadcasts on the go. It had been hugely popular. For exactly three and a half months. Then Dewey never saw a single person use it again. Except as a non-verbal protest against his presence.

Then there was the schoolgirl, outside Ofuna on the Tokkaido Line, probably about fourteen, who spent twenty-five minutes looking at him in awe, like she'd seen a god. Of course, that had been his interpretation of her unending gaze.

Dewey glanced over and caught sight of the guy's clothes. He was dressed in an AKB48 T-shirt. Appropriate for this kind of weather. The man's skin was covered with blotches of red. Rashes and infections everywhere.

He had been told with great authority by Yuko, one of his coworkers in Shinjuku, that thirty per cent of all Japanese had some form of skin disease. Of course, most never got it treated. To see a doctor meant they had to pay thirty per cent of the bill. If, and only if, they had a job of some sort. Many unemployed didn't bother paying their government health insurance premiums. Since there was no legal way to compel them to do so.

It meant they couldn't go to a hospital. You were only compelled to pay for insurance if you worked more than thirty hours a week, with your employer paying half. If you worked less, you had to buy a different kind of government coverage, called 'citizens health insurance.' Which got quite a bit more expensive after an initial few years, with premiums that always went up for reasons Dewey couldn't explain.

The bottom line was many people in Japan didn't go to the doctor, almost all of them poor. So on trains, especially outside central Tokyo, people tended to look a lot rougher. It was almost the opposite of the United States, where the destitute were gathered in the inner cities, close to shelters and charities. He always heard the Brits and Canadians complaining about rough looking Japanese.

Dewey had at least been able to score a window seat. On the local trains there was no reserved seating. They were traveling right along the ocean. On the wrong side of Japan, as they called it in Tokyo and Osaka. The Sea of Japan coast. It wasn't really fair to say this. Just that, coincidentally, all the cities with most of the country's wealth were on the Pacific side.

The weather was a lot worse up here, too. Along Honshu and Kyushu they weren't spared the disgusting humid summers that prevailed from June to early September. Despite this, these same places suffered a far worse winter. Cold Siberian winds passed over the sea, collecting moisture. When this mass of cold, wet air hit the mountains in central Japan, they released the moisture as snow, blanketing the northwest coast. Before continuing on as cold, dry air to the other side of the country. While the Pacific coast might see little more than flurries once or twice a winter, the Sea of Japan often saw considerable accumulations. Sometimes several meters of wet snow in a single winter. Enough to make life miserable.

Still, it was an incredible place to travel by train. The tracks were carved into the side of a cliff. Occasionally passing by a lonely house, where some brave soul had decided to tough it out. From Dewey's window it was a straight drop to the sea. Looking down, he could only see water. Of course, the view of the horizon was obscured by giant pillars. Upon which rested the Hokuriku Expressway. Rising out of the ocean on concrete pylons. Dewey wondered what would happen if a major quake struck. You'd have no place to jump, except the ocean.

An earthquake had struck about ten years earlier in Niigata. Almost took out the nuclear power plant. Japan seemed to enjoy rolling the dice when it came to atomic energy. All in a bid for increased self-sufficiency. That was how the country operated, thought Dewey, keep doing what you're doing until you walk right into catastrophe.

Staring out at the sea, he wondered if they'd passed into Yamagata from Niigata prefecture. The route he'd planned wouldn't take him to Yamagata city, so there was no way of knowing. It would still be several hours to Akita, to the hot spring town that was his final destination.

Another house caught Dewey's eye. A brightly colored chalet, looking like it had been transplanted from the Alps of Switzerland. His glance drifted to the twitchy guy. Their eyes met briefly. The man had anger welled up beneath his gaze. He looked down at the guy's sweatpants. Country clothing for the rural poor. The man had a small backpack by his feet.

Dewey felt needling in his right abdomen. Twitchy guy's elbow. The train turned away from the sea, towards a valley of rice fields. They passed through a tunnel. The elbowing got worse. Why? What compelled him to behave this way? The man could have sat anywhere.

Finally Dewey couldn't stand it anymore. "Excuse me," he said in Japanese, "could you please put your elbow down?" He pointed to his waist. "You're hitting me right here. Stop, please."

The guy immediately retracted his arms. Dewey's foreign language ability was far from perfect, but it had done the job. The guy hadn't expected the foreigner to say anything, let alone in Japanese. Dewey had noticed such behavior in his four years living in Tokyo. People often felt free to behave badly because most Japanese, at least in East Japan, put up with them, or tried to ignore such transgressions.

Then the muttering started. Rapid-fire. Like a whisper, under twitchy guy's breath. Like he was chanting. Dewey looked over. The guy's eyes were closed. It was really creepy. Dewey tried to lean towards the window, as far away as possible. Letting the sound of the tracks drown everything else out.

Just when Dewey felt he could no longer bear it, twitchy guy got up and left. For the moment. Dewey noticed he'd left his backpack and sneakers behind. The train emerged from the tunnel. Rice fields all around. The announcement for the next station came on.

A rush of air blew through the compartment. Someone had opened both doors connecting the train cars.

From above came a bunch of clomps. Like a horse was walking on the top of the train.

They hit a straightaway. The train slowed abruptly. An automated announcement came on in Japanese. Dewey couldn't really understand it, because he'd only heard it twice before, in his entire four years living here. But he was pretty sure what it was before the chipper female voice came on in English: "The emergency brakes have been applied. Please grab hold of a hand strap or railing to prevent injury from sudden deceleration."

Someone had jumped in front of the train.

They would be here for a while. Waiting for the police to arrive.

2

Every seat on the Yamagata shinkansen had been booked. The Joetsu one, too. In fact, all the bullet trains heading to Hokuriku were reserved well in advance. Which came as a shock to Dewey. Those two lines, along with the Akita and Yamagata shinkansens, were regarded as the white elephants of Japanese infrastructure. Built during the eighties when Japan was rolling in it. The government doubled down. The Niigata shinkansen would open soon, completing a loop of money-losing high-speed train service to places no one wanted to go.

And yet, they were booked solid for all of Golden Week. To understand why, it has to be understood that the entire country of Japan goes on vacation at the same time. A cultural shock to most Americans. There were three main travel periods. New Year's, which went from the first of January to the first Monday of the following week. Unlike North Americans, most Japanese treat Christmas as a holiday to see one's boyfriend or girlfriend, while New Year's Day is considered more solemn, and reserved for family activities.

After that came Golden Week—three consecutive statutory holidays, with a fourth that fell with a workday between it and the other three. At Dewey's company the language instructors got the entire week off. Fortunately.

Then, in the middle of August came obon (pronounced OH-BONE, something that took Dewey years to master). While there were no statutory holidays on the calendar, virtually the entire country took at least a week off in the middle of the month.

During these periods all flights, trains and highways were packed. Even money losing routes like the Joetsu and Nagano shinkansens. Hell, they weren't even proper bullet trains.

They ran on conventional rails, just a little bit faster, unlike the Tokkaido line, which was grade separated on special tracks. And the Joetsu line didn't even go to Joetsu. It terminated at Niigata city.

Dewey stared out his window. In the distance he caught a glimpse of flashing red lights. The police were on scene now. This sort of thing happened every week in Tokyo. There were even times, often near the bi-yearly bonus seasons, when trains were stopped every day. By "human body fall accidents." Salarymen jumping to claim life insurance benefits. Some of the private rail companies had gotten wise to this and started going after the families of suicide victims. Compensation for the costs in timetable disruption and clean up.

Dewey had been delayed no less than five times by jumpers in the last eight months. Usually on a Wednesday, just after lunch. People just couldn't hack it. Isolated and alone. Couldn't make it to the weekend. Lunch in Japan is a full sixty minutes, by law, at all companies. A time when coworkers socialize and gossip. The embarrassment of not belonging to a group has driven some employees, and often university students, to have their lunches in bathroom stalls. To avoid the stigma of eating alone. Some don't make it back to work, preferring hara-kiri by rail line and rolling stock.

Then there was the salaryman who had jumped in front of a Marunochi Line train one afternoon. In a spectacularly ill-timed attempt, this individual had bounced off the front car of the train. His entire weight bounced back onto the platform, nailing an innocent bystander full bore. Dewey didn't know if the person on the platform had lived or not.

Feeling a bit hungry, Dewey reached up and grabbed his backpack. He had stuffed it full with toiletries and clothing. An attempt to pack as lightly as possible. In the front compartment he found a small plastic bag from 7-11. Inside, a bottle of green tea and a package of dried squid strips. While they had potato chips and chocolate bars, Dewey had gone to the effort of sampling the local snack foods. The green tea was sugarless, naturally almost free of calories.

He'd arrived in Osaka two nights previous. With all the trains booked, he'd bought a seishin jyuuhachi kippu (pronounced SAY-SHEEN-JEW-HA-CHEE... oh, fuck it. It's not important), a long-winded name for a train ticket that made far more sense in the original kanji. It allowed a full day's travel on any local train run by Japan Railways. Unfortunately that meant no shinkansens or reserved seats. But you got five days of transport, which you could share with friends. All for little more than twenty dollars a day. A pretty good deal.

On the second day, Dewey had made his way to Niigata. Despite having a population of over three quarters of a million people, it had made almost no impression on him. If you had to pick a generic place in Japan, you could do no more unremarkable than Niigata City. The usual collection of overpriced department stores. Hocking luxury handbags. The usual chains of izakayas, coffee shops, and fast food restaurants. Although Dewey had heard the sake was quite good. Ample access to rice and decent water.

On his way there Dewey had a layover for half an hour in Joetsu. It was probably the most depressing place he'd ever been. A crumbling town of old buildings and even older people. What is this country going to do? he wondered. The elderly were a financial time bomb. The countryside was hollowing out. Soon every city of less than two million people was going to look like Joetsu. Ugly wooden buildings slowly being ravaged away by the elements.

It was the kind of thing that dissuaded Dewey from putting down roots here.

He'd started working for the ABC Language Academy four years ago. They almost never gave much of a raise, but they were generous in allotting more vacation days the longer you stayed. Which, in some ways, was better.

In Japan both the school and the work year start at the beginning of April. Despite the recent push to change them to September. So you began a new schedule of classes, and within a month you had a vacation—Golden Week. So named by movie theater owners after the golden profits the statutory holidays delivered. If the spring holidays were timed just right, as they were this year, people would end up with an entire week off. Most years people went back to work for a day after the first holiday, then got three more days to hit the road. Now people were pushing to add a fourth day. Make it a full week.

Despite getting some extra time this year, Dewey's vacation was, unfortunately, doomed. Bibi and everything else going on was making him miserable. How had things gotten this way? He wasn't a weak man. The wrong girl had come into his life. Now said girl was gone. Until this trip. Because of workplace bullshit. He should have gone to Hawaii.

Something caught his attention outside. Two police. Carrying a stretcher, draped in a blue tarp. Walking on the narrow embankment by the tracks.

The man carrying the front end of the stretcher slipped.

The tarp fell off, revealing a mass of red and black. Something rolled off, like a basketball, coming to rest below Dewey's window.

The basketball had a face.

The twitchy guy. The locomotive had cut his head clean off.

3

Two hours later, the train resumed its journey.

According to one of Dewey's colleagues in Tokyo, the police had to identify and mark the location of each piece of human remains. Just in case it turned out not to be a suicide. In the capital region, investigators had it down pat, clearing a site in about forty minutes. But this wasn't Tokyo.

Dewey finished off his squid strips, and hungered for more. Regretted not buying an onigiri or a sandwich.

The next section of the journey took Dewey away from the ocean. Past endless rice fields. Watching the entirety of the country's staple sustenance fly by. Japan imported plenty of food, but not rice. And the government paid farmers real well to maintain that supply. It was a long journey, with many unexpected stops now that the schedule was disrupted. Hours later the train pulled into Sakata station in Akita.

It was a forty-five minute wait for the next departure to Kita-Yamanouchi. Dewey was starving. Walking through town, he passed by nothing but abandoned stores. Long since closed down. He headed back to the station. In the convenience store next to the waiting area he found nothing left on the refrigerated shelves but a lone egg salad sandwich. It would have to do.

The final departure of the day was a small two-car train that looked about eighty years old. He really was heading to the edge of civilization. A far cry from the ten-car trains of the Yamanote Line. At least it wasn't crowded. He counted no more than half a dozen people on board. Weathered farmers and a couple of school children. The train only ran seven times each day. Dewey was lucky he hadn't missed it.

As night fell, his cell phone's battery died. Dewey had three more hours to go. He fell asleep. When he awoke the train was almost there, pulling into the second-last station. After departing, they entered a tunnel for the final leg of the journey. It must have taken twenty minutes to pass through it all. In Japan this wasn't unusual. It reminded him of the train heading into Nagasaki. The feeling of a place cut off from the rest of the world. Almost.

Kita-Yamanouchi. "Kita" as in north. "Yama" meant mountain. "no" was the connecting particle. "uchi" was Japanese for innermost. This place must be inside the mountains. But as the train came to rest at the final stop, the first thing Dewey saw out his window was a harbor. Strange. He hadn't expected to be so close to the water.

Dewey disembarked. He was the only passenger who wasn't a high school student. Out beyond the platform was a small village. Nestled in darkness. He looked up at the platform clock. Five minutes after ten. Late. Dewey took out his wallet. He needed money. All he had left was the equivalent of thirty-five dollars in cash.

He found a 7-11 next to the station. Went right up to the ATM. After checking that it did, in fact, take Mitsubishi-UFJ bank cards, he attempted to make a withdrawal. He was then greeted by a message that informed him the machine was only operational between the hours of eight in the morning until ten at night.

This was trouble. He had no money. And he had no map. After wandering the streets for fifteen minutes, he found the Yamanoki Ryokan. This was where Megumi had booked them in. He walked into the genkan. The place looked dark the only sign of life the far off noise of a television. Dewey knocked on the wall next to the shelves where people put their shoes.

"Hello?" he yelled in English.

A figure appeared at the end of the hall. "Good evening," said the aging woman in Japanese.

Dewey switched languages. "I'm really sorry I'm late." He explained his situation on the train.

"Yes," said the women, "It is regrettable, but we cancel reservations after nine o'clock. The only room we have left is the larger one. Unfortunately it costs a great deal more."

"Yes," he said, "but I might have a problem paying." He explained about his bank card. "But I'll give you cash first thing tomorrow morning."

"Do you have a credit card?"

"Not one that works in Japan."

From the woman's silence Dewey gathered that she was pissed. But it wouldn't be good manners to turn him out on the street. There were no other hotels or hostels in the village. It was this place or a bench on the train platform.

After a long awkward pause she nodded and beckoned him in. He was led down a narrow hallway. Then up to an enormous second floor room. It could have slept an entire family, easily.

"How much is this?" he asked.

She quoted him a number that was more than a third of the monthly rent on his Tokyo apartment.

Dewey nodded. What other choice did he have? There went his savings. "Is there any way I could order something to eat?"

"I'm sorry," she said, "but we've finished dinner service."

After an awkward pause, during which Dewey realized that getting information out of this woman would be like pulling teeth, he asked, "Is there any place around here that serves food?"

"There is an izakaya next door."

"Thank you."

After settling in, Dewey went out to explore the town. The place next door turned out to be a yakitori restaurant. He was too tired to guess what the strange kanjis on the menu meant, so he continued on.

Everything on the main street was closed. Not a surprise. In many of these country places, everything shuts down at six o'clock. Dewey turned the corner by the train station. Right above him was an illuminated sign. An authentic Irish pub. In the middle of nowhere. And it was open. Unbelievable.

The interior was a perfect imitation of a public house one might find in Cork or Galway. And completely deserted. From the kitchen he heard someone greeting him in Japanese. The moment the man saw Dewey, he switched to English. "What can I get for you?"

"You speak English," said Dewey.

"Of course, everyone in this town speaks it perfectly. It's the law."

4

"You're joking," said Dewey.

"No," said the man. "It is all to attract more tourists to our village. We got a special loan to open this bar."

Dewey looked around. "It's very authentic."

"Will you have a drink?"

"Yes, how about a pint of Rogue Amber?"

"Sure." The bartender grabbed a glass.

"And do you have a food menu?"

"Right here."

"My god," said Dewey, looking at the long list of dishes. "I'll try the haggis."

"A very good choice."

"How long have you studied English for? I've never met anyone who speaks it so well, not even in Roppongi."

The man laughed and passed over the drink. "That's five hundred yen." Dewey passed him a coin. The man yelled into the kitchen in Japanese, then turned back. "Our mayor is very proactive here. He wants to spur economic development. Part of that is making our village more accessible to tourists. He wants to have a one hundred per cent bilingual population in the next five years."

Dewey sipped his beer. "That's quite ambitious."

"It is. But it's been effective so far." The man wiped the bar. "Also, this week is one of our major events."

"What's that?"

"The two day march."

"Oh yeah, I've heard of those. Kind of like a marathon, right?"

"Something like that. Will you be here for a while?"

"Yeah. Until next week."

"I see." The bartender poured himself a small draft of beer. "What do you do in Tokyo?"

"I'm an English teacher."

The bartender smiled. Dewey expected that most foreigners who came in here said the same thing. "You work at an eikaiwa?"

"Yes. The ABC Language Academy. You've heard of it?"

The man nodded. "One of my friends took lessons there as a child."

"Did they learn much?"

"Nope. Nothing."

"Yeah, it's pretty much useless for most of the people who come through the door. There's no way you're going to learn anything if you come in once or twice a week. I guess they see it as a hobby. I also teach at a women's university twice a week."

"Lots of pretty girls."

"You'd think, but it feels a lot like a glorified high school. I mean, the girls are nice. But they all seem to blend into one big mass of femaleness. I like to be with a girl who stands out."

"Do you like Japanese girls?"

"Sure. But I don't think they like me."

The bartender laughed. "Some girls are very difficult. Many can get money by working at a hostess club."

"Yeah," said Dewey, "that would never fly back home. In America the only people who are paid to look pretty are models and prostitutes."

"But the little cute girls? They look innocent, but they are not. Many of them like to have sex."

"I'll bet." Dewey mused that a tall girl wouldn't have many potential suitors in this country.

"So," asked the bartender, "why did you come to Japan?"

Ahh, thought Dewey, the inescapable question at every first encounter with a Japanese person. He at least gave the guy credit for taking so long to get to it. Usually it was the first question he was asked. Then the one about Japanese girls. "Well," said Dewey, finishing his drink and indicating his desire for another one, "I moved back to Santa Barbara after college. Couldn't find any job in finance. So I decided to come here. That was right after the financial crisis. Been here four years."

"Do you want to stay?"

"Not sure. Hard to make money living in Tokyo, the cost of rent is high."

The bartender approached with another pint of beer. Dewey couldn't believe it was so cheap. "Another Rogue Amber." He took the 500 yen coin. "How is it?"

Dewey took a sip. "Excellent. I can't believe you have all these beers on tap."

"It's our specialty. Many Americans come here for it. Some from as far away as Sendai and Aomori. Many of them are English teachers."

"Yeah. It's not a very good job if you like money. But you get a lot of free time. I feel bad for those salarymen who have to work really hard, but get only one day a week off. It must be awful."

"It is. I used to be one of those," said the bartender. "Every day I would work from eight-thirty in the morning until midnight. And on two Saturdays every month."

"Yeah, you never see that in America."

The bartender smiled. "There is an American who comes in here many nights."

"Oh yeah? Where's he from?"

"Texas, I believe."

"Yeah, the U.S. has really gone to the dogs. Ever since Obama got in. He's the one who caused all this mess. After all those people fighting in Iraq. This is their reward. I think Rand Paul is our only hope. He knows what's going on. I'm willing to bet he'll be the next president."

"Why? Do you like President Bush?"

"Hell no. He was stupid. Spending all this money on his friends. Telling everyone what to do. Looking through library books to catch terrorists. And for what? They found two guys in ten years. But every bureaucrat and cop loves him. Every single one got a boost in salary. Spending their time pretending to look for terrorists. My ass!"

"Bush was not popular in Japan. People like Obama because in Fukui—"

"Yeah, I passed through the town yesterday."

"Did you try the Echizen soba? It is very famous."

"No, maybe next time."

A bell rang. The bartender grabbed Dewey's dinner from the kitchen. The plate was steaming hot. He had never had haggis before. It was like a kind of meatloaf, except spicy. A bit dry, but it was good.

When Dewey was done eating the bartender approached. "You should come to the march on Friday."

"I don't know. My traveling companions are arriving that afternoon."

"Really? Other teachers?"

"One of them. The other two are eikaiwa staff. All girls."

"How exciting. Do they like to go hiking?"

"No idea. I doubt the Japanese girls are into it. They seemed excited to come visit the onsen. Don't know about the other one."

"Is she American, too?"

"Nope. Swedish."

"A blond girl?"

"Very blond."

"Is she your girlfriend?"

Dewey paused. This was awkward. "No. She likes to date Japanese guys. Likes their skin."

The bartender laughed. "You should hook up me."

"Hook you up? Sure. I'm more gunning for her Japanese friend anyway."

About the author

Shane O'Brien MacDonald was born in 1980 on Cape Breton Island in eastern Canada. He speaks English, Japanese, and Chinese, and has a degree in economics and film studies from Queen's University. Before becoming a novelist he worked as an editor, cinematographer, and assistant picture editor on dozens of films and television shows. He has also been a foreign language instructor at the Tokyo University of Agriculture.

Mr. MacDonald is the author of the Kiki Claymore series of books, which have been described as "post-Ian Fleming female-centric espionage comic books in novel form."